RINGING FOR YOU

Anouchka Grose Forrester was born in Sydney in 1970. She moved to London aged two and has lived there ever since.

RINGING
FOR YOU

Anouchka Grose Forrester

Flamingo
An Imprint of HarperCollins*Publishers*

Flamingo
An Imprint of HarperCollins*Publishers*
77-85 Fulham Palace Road,
Hammersmith, London W6 8JB

Flamingo is a registered trade mark of
HarperCollins Publishers Limited

www.**fireandwater**.com

Published by Flamingo 2000
1 3 5 7 9 8 6 4 2

First published in Great Britain by
Flamingo 1999

This novel is entirely a work of fiction.
The names, characters and incidents portrayed in it are
the work of the author's imagination. Any resemblance to
actual persons, living or dead, events or localities is
entirely coincidental.

Author photograph by Patricio Grose Forrester

ISBN 0 00 655156 4

Set in Galliard

Printed and bound in Great Britain by
Caledonian International Book Manufacturing Ltd, Glasgow

FOR PATRICIO

ACKNOWLEDGMENTS

Thanks to all the people who helped along the way, especially to Darian Leader for his encouragement and astute tips, Julian Loose for reassurance at an early stage, Jonny Geller for his support and excellent last-minute advice, Rachel Hore for making more reception jobs unnecessary, Jennifer Parr for being a generous editor, Roslyn and Peter Grose for never telling me to get a proper job and to Patricio Grose Forrester for being who he is.

What is stupider than a receptionist? So stupid that no one dares offer her discourse publicly without a serious mediation: novel, play, or analysis (between tweezers).

Adapted from Roland Barthes

CONTENTS

INTRODUCTION

It's normal when you're reading to expect a few false starts. I never feel like I've started a book until I've read at least twenty pages. So the bit you're reading now, you're probably not really getting. Never mind. If you find yourself unmoved for the moment, perhaps you'll realize later how necessary all this was.

I don't mind admitting that I haven't got everything fully worked out yet – to tell you the truth, I've no idea how it's going to end up. All I can say for sure right now is that it's going to be cheap. I'm going to do the best I can with what I've got lying around. The characters will be borrowed from my life and from the human bargain-basement that is my office. They won't take any cruises or buy expensive dresses. There won't even be any dramatic weather. I know I could add some extravagant meals or country houses at no extra cost to myself, but I just don't feel like it. This is going to be a no frills novel.

I wonder what you'd like to know first. There is a famous argument between two famous writers (so famous that I've forgotten both their names) about the best way to start a book. One of them thought that you should go straight in with the interesting stuff, to get the reader hooked, and then go back and sort out the boring stuff later. The other one was much more in favour of the 'I was born in . . .' type beginning because, having got the tedious bit over with, it was uphill all the way. The first one sort of won, in that most books these days try to start as interesting as possible. But I quite sympathize with the other guy (it's always more fun to back the loser). Still, if

1

it's possible, I'd rather try a bit of both because I don't feel like taking sides on such a difficult issue. I'll keep quiet about my hair colour and all that – this isn't an 0898 number. Perhaps I could begin by telling you how come I have enough time to write. I'm a receptionist and am obliged to sit still for hours on the trot. I'm sure you know that sitting still for too long can make you feel pretty bad. It's unhealthy to have so much time to think. I've been reading quite a bit myself – in the hope of distracting myself away from my own problems – but it's not really helping. Hearing about other people's fascinating lives is reminding me of all the things I'd rather be doing than answering the telephone at the Academy of Material Science – a sleepy organization whose commendable aim is to spread information about engineering products and ideas.

In order to give you a better picture of what things are like for me I'll keep writing as if all I'm doing is writing, but every time the telephone rings I'll make a little sign (☎) so at least you know the extent to which my attention is divided. Maybe your phone will ring while you're reading and drag you away for a few hours, or even forever.

⌣

I know. As I can't decide which nameless famous writer to back, I'll hurry things along a bit by giving you a brief list of what you can expect later. If you carry on reading you will come across:

The sad story of my lonely first birthday

The ins and outs of my frustrating and imperfect lovelife ☎

A few cod-philosophical spiels about this and that (I'm sorry about this part, but I just can't help myself)

A story which starts ☎ slowly, gradually builds up to a devastating crescendo and then stays there for a while (I'm being rather optimistic with that last bit but I assure you, at least, that I will somehow find a way to stop being a receptionist

2

and learn some useful truths about life and love before your very eyes)

(*I think I'll have to have a second symbol to show when I'm signing for a package:* ✍.)

You will also meet over thirty very compelling (though inexpensive) ☎ characters – some only superficially and some in intimate detail.

Ultimately I'd like to work out something about my first birthday catastrophe and how it may offer vital clues to why my present romantic situation is so disastrous (although I can't yet work out exactly why I think so). If I can do this then all the sitting still and stewing in my own juices won't have been a complete waste of time ☎.

⤺

All those ☎s are making me lose concentration. I'll tell you what the average ☎ is like so you can appreciate what a hassle they are. The call is signalled by a moany sounding bleep and a small, flashing red light. I push the button under the red light and pick up the handset. Then I say, 'Good morning, (or afternoon) Academy of Material Science,' without getting the words all bunched together so that the caller has to ask me to repeat it, and without saying it so slowly that the person gets bored and interrupts before I finish. Then I try to work out what they want, which is sometimes easy and sometimes hard. Often they don't know it themselves, or can't remember or pronounce the name of the person they need. Sometimes they just say 'errr' for a bit before getting to the point. Sometimes they really go for the jugular and ask a polysyllabic material science type question which I have to confess to not being able to answer, causing them to treat me like a thicko and to start calling me Miss. Whatever, having got a grip on who they need, I look up the extension number on a flaky old list covered in little gashes where my frustrated predecessors have stabbed it with their pencils. Then I type this number into the heat-sensitive, fingertip-shaped indentations on the board and check the digital panel to see whether the person is engaged, engaged with a call waiting or diverted to another line. Then I tell the caller what the situation is and see what they want to do – hold, try later or leave a message (all of which are annoying). Unless the phone just rings unproblematically, in which case I say, 'It's ringing' (I don't actually say 'for you' because it sounds too receptionisty) or just, 's'ringing' and get off the line as quickly as possible before the other person picks up. So what might look like just a little ☎ to you – mildly irritating but easy to ignore – is a giant pain in the arse for me. I'm aware that the signs may start to bother you, but I'd really rather you knew about the calls as, unfortunately, they form a major component of my existence.

1

All About Me

I'll tell you the main thing you need to know about me, after which everything else will be subsidiary. This is the lens through which you'll need to look to understand all my actions. I've always been someone who would probably describe themself as happy. But equally I've always gone around with a strong sense of something being badly missing. I think I'm pretty normal in this respect. For me the missing bit has always seemed rather overpowering and ruined a lot of stuff that wasn't necessarily deserving of ruination (especially romantic stuff). However, as a feeling, I can say with a huge amount of certainty that I'd rather not be without it. It's sort of like the glitter on a Christmas card – the picture would be pretty average without it, but the glitter comes along and makes it look special.

Just for the sake of giving it some sort of historical dignity, I'll tell you how I think this feeling got there in the first place. ☎ It had always been around, but nothing had really forced me to recognize it until one day, at the age of seventeen, I found myself reading a slightly tedious book about child development. It had a chapter on parental disappearance and its effects on the infant (based on the theories of a man called John Bowlby which, so it said, anyone in their right mind agrees are largely crap). The effects were divided into three stages: initially the child would be sad, angry and sorry for itself and wonder what it had done wrong (the first five days or so), then it would be miserable for a bit but cry a lot less and not so convincingly, and finally (in the space of a fortnight) it would become really cheerful, although obviously detached, and start forming easy relationships with whoever was around. The child's character ☎ would be formed according to which stage of desolation the baby was in on the parents' return. The theory applies to children up to the age of five, after which they can supposedly sort out their problems without too much trouble. The whole process took two weeks, meaning that a child abandoned for a fortnight would be capable of fantastic feats of overcoming pain and upset – while not actually overcoming them at all. In other words, it would learn how to behave as if nothing was wrong in situations where it quite clearly was. It would detach itself from the agony while remaining agonized by the detachment. And, as if that weren't enough, on the parents' return, after a period of clinging, dependent behaviour, it would become 'attention seeking, uninhibited, indiscriminately friendly' and quickly ☎ develop (in the words of a Mr M. Rutter) 'a personality characterized by lack of guilt, an inability to keep to rules and an inability to form lasting relationships'. Something in the description struck a chord with me (a whole Beatles songbook actually) but as far as I knew I had no history of abandonment, so I decided to put the experience down to the rampant identifications one is bound to undergo when reading psychology books.

Still, this particular account seemed to have more potency than all the other empathies I suffered at the time, and I began to wonder whether the ☎ same effects could be rendered by a different set of circumstances (like Capricorns who, on reading all the other – more appropriate – horoscopes, start to ask whether they have Scorpio rising or the moon in Leo).

Ages later, when searching through an old photo album and grappling with the unbelievable notion that *I* was once a baby – *that* baby, even, in *that* picture, with the Pekinese hairstyle and smock – I stumbled across a postcard. The front was quite repellent and I felt no particular urge to read it. It just didn't look very interesting. It didn't seem up to the task of diverting my gaze away from the infinitely more captivating photographs of *me*. It was white with a blue cod-Victorian swirly border framing the words '*Defense d'Uriner*' in large black curling letters. Don't ask how, but something about it nonetheless must have caught my attention. It sort of by-passed my normal decision-making faculties and got permission from a higher authority. It caught me unawares and I found myself switched imperceptibly from uninterested to irrevocably mesmerized. The more I looked at it the more its cringing miserableness took on an ineffable power. Steadily, inscrutably, it became more and more repulsive until I realized I was going to have to read it. The back was covered with my mother's scrawly writing. I scanned it quickly to see what it was and where it was from and was appalled to see that it was addressed to 'Darling . . .' – my name! and shamelessly proclaimed 'Happy First Birthday!'.

The other day on the news there was a feature about a postcard that took eighty years to reach its destination. Apparently it fell behind a filing cabinet at the post office in 1916 and had to wait until the building was refurbished in 1996 to complete the final leg of its journey. The intended recipients had long since died and the new homeowners were somewhat surprised. Naturally they saw the funny side and didn't feel too spooked. When my postcard finally arrived, however, I was outraged. It was a first birthday card from my mother in Barbados, sent to me in London, where I was busy being shunted back and forth between my two grannies.

She'd abandoned me and never mentioned it and all the stuff in the psychology book was exactly right. I was arrested for shoplifting shortly before receiving the card, and, in accordance with the prediction, found it very hard to act guilty at the police station. Why would I feel bad? I was simply a half-grown-up abandoned baby acting out the effects of my early trauma in the designated manner. I had also been booted out of school for my attention-seeking hairstyle and had developed a serious compulsion to befriend tramps, public schoolboys, prostitutes, ageing architects, lost tourists, blind people and anyone else who crossed my path. They would fail to understand that my friend-liness was merely the product of a bad day I'd had a number of years back and didn't actually mean I liked them. They would ring me or buzz the entryphone at my family home only to be told, by me or my well-practised parents, that I no longer lived there. However, far from being an out-of-control teenager, I was behaving in absolute obedience to the rules laid out before me at the tender age of one. And at last, already having become the thing I was destined to turn into, I found myself confronted by the object that announced my fate. My parents had gone on holiday for a month, missed my first birthday, and sent me a card forbidding me to pee.

∽

I just have to interrupt this heartrending account of childhood trauma to say that by a miracle of space/time transformation, in the time it took you to pass from the last sentence to this one (a hundredth of a second?) a whole day has elapsed for me.

∽

All this might not sound like much of a big deal to you, but you have to understand that for me, having lived with the effects of my parents' ☎ month-long disappearance for twenty or so years, it was quite a discovery. My 'character' no longer seemed to me an indistinct mass of uneasy combinations, but a perfectly functioning mechanism doing quite flawlessly what it had been programmed to do. I asked my mother about it and she was quite surprised that I attached so much significance to the event. She said she'd never told me because she didn't think it mattered. When I pushed the point she got all shirty and said she'd never planned that my first birthday would be on the fourth of February. What a dodgy argument. My mum

8

is nice, but we're very alike. I sort of suspect that her mum and dad might have done a similar thing to her, which would explain why she refuses to feel guilty about it. At least my dad got quite remorseful when I asked him and said he had often worried that some of the less fun parts of my personality might have come about as a direct result of their vacation. He said it in this gawky way though that made me suspect he was going along with me just to be kind. Whenever you start a conversation like this with him, he'll play along with you for a bit and then switch to talking to the dog. I really love my parents (not quite as crazily as when I was little and I used to lie at the bottom of the front door like a draught excluder, waiting for them to get back from their dinner parties) but I find it really hard to talk about feelings with them.

My mum looks a bit like Helen Mirren and my dad is a kind of Steve Martin type, only more English. They're definitely a handsome couple. She used to work in TV but she stopped when she turned fifty and became a marriage guidance counsellor. My dad is an inventor, working mostly with petro-chemicals. He generally has a lot of financial problems because inventing can be an unreliable business. His trouble seems to be that he does it more for love than for money, which means that he carries on working on things, even if he can't get any funding. My mum is very understanding, but I think it's no accident that she's become a bit of an expert in the field of saving shaky relationships. They live in the middle of a field in Norfolk, but I was born and brought up in London.

☎ So now you know; I'm a bit fucked, but at least there's a reason for it – and actually I'm quite pleased. It's so neat. And now that we're a bit better acquainted I don't mind telling you that I have waist-length blonde ringlets.

9

2

A Bit About Other People

So, having vaguely established who I am, we can talk about some other things. But there's one serious obstacle to overcome. I'd wanted to borrow one of my friends' characters as a writing aid (well, yes, I was planning to nick it). He has – without realizing – absolutely forbidden me from doing so ☎. I think it's very unfair and absolutely incomprehensible. I'd be so thrilled to be turned into a literary character by almost anyone (even myself). But he doesn't feel the same way. (He clearly doesn't suffer the same lack of guilt and careless exhibitionism.) The stupid part of it is that he's always taking pictures of people – sometimes of me – but he seems to think photographs are different to stories, that they somehow give less away. He doesn't like me to mention him to my friends, ☎ which I can sort of understand (some of my better friends are highly practised meddlers and vicious gossips). He hates it with such a passion that I know I can't write about him. Which is a pain as he is one of the central characters in my life (at least for now – people like me aren't meant to have lasting central characters, remember?). This, I'm afraid is going to cause problems initially, but I'm sure there's a way to deal with the ☎ obstruction. From now on, wherever necessary, we will refer to him as the man who mustn't be mentioned, or the MWMM, or perhaps merely the ∧∧∧∧, and just try to work around the fact that he can't quite properly be here. I'm bored with this train of thought. It doesn't even deserve the word train – maybe it's more of ☎☎☎☎ (wow!) an adjustable roller-skate.

I would like today to be a full-distance writing marathon. ☎ Only I've just looked at the meetings schedule and realized that I'm going to have to smile and say ☎ ✍ something nice and give badges and directions to one hundred and three people in six different meetings in different rooms at different times. And for self-evident reasons I find the prospect quite distressing. Partly because a hundred and three people are about to treat me like a rec ☎☎✍☎eptionist and partly because, while I'm folding their little names into little plastic wallets, telling them where the 'cloakroom' is (I'm the ☎ ☎ least embarrassing person to ask because I have the least power and am therefore supposedly sympathetic to their powerlessness in the face of their bodily functions), pointing them in the right direction, estimating their chances of being given coffee, etc., it's a little bit hard to take myself seriously as a great writer. (I'm going to need a new sign for these human interruptions: ✗ .) I've been forgetting to note some of the packages because I actually quite like it when they ✗ come. The people who bring them are generally pretty ✗ ✗ ✗ ✗ reasonable ✗ ✗ and it doesn't feel so much like an interruption – more like something actually happening (even if all it is is signing a piece of paper and making a facile joke). It does make me wonder what the exact difference is between something ✗ standing up on its own as a thing that happens, ✗ and something that doesn't appear to have its own force and intrinsic justification but just seems like a ✗ ✗ ✗ ✗ nuisance ✗ ✗ that ✗ ✗ ✗ ✗ ✗ ✗ ✗ ✗ comes bursting in. I actually just interrupted myself ☎✗ and went out for a ☎☎☎✍☎☎ ✍✗ ✗ ✗ ✍ cigarette. Smoking is my favourite interruption at the moment. I just ✗ started doing it again ✗ ✗ ✗ ✗ ✍ when I met ☎☎ the ✗ ✗ ✗ ☎☎✗ ✗ ☎ ∿∿∿. I really love it and can't remember at all why I ever ✗ ✗ ✗ ✗ ✗ thought it was so important to stop. If I have

11

nothing to thank him for ✂ ✂ ✂ ☎ ☎ ✂ ☎ ✂ ☎ ☎ ✂ in the end, I'll ✂ ☎ ✂ ✂ ✂ ☎ ☎ find it somehow in my heart to be grateful for all the cigarettes I've enjoyed. ✂ ☎ I'm ✂ ✂ fed up with all the stuff happening around me now and would really like ✂ ✂ ✂ ✂ ✂ ✂ ✂ ✍ to switch it ✂ off and think about something ✂ ✂ ✂ ✂ completely different. Maybe we could go back to the problem of character and ask what ☎ ✂ it means to pinch someone else's for the purpose of writing. What if I kept ✂ ☎✍ it to my feelings about him and his effect on me (and maybe a few unimportant facts and details that wouldn't give away his identity or get him in trouble with anyone)? Would that still be somehow his property? Obviously not, I'd say, but I don't know how much I'd ✂ ✂ ✂ ✂ ✂ ✍✂ ✂ like him to know about all that. Assuming he'll read this, which is actually quite unlikely. The whole game I play with him depends entirely on his not knowing it. ✂ ☎✂ ☎✂ And I worry that if I play the game and win ✂ ✂ ✂ ✂ ✂ (he falls completely in love with me) ✂ ✂ ✂ ✍☎☎✂ ✂ and then he finds out later the thoughts and feelings governing my ☎ (I hope) inexplicable ✂ ☎☎✂ actions, all the good ☎☎✂ ✂ ✂ ✂ ✂ ✂ work ☎✂ I've done ✂ ✂ ✂ ☎✂ ✂ will be completely destroyed by my having made myself pathetically transparent. ✂ ✂ ✂ ☎✂ ✂ ✂ ✂ ✍✂ ✂

(Against all the odds I made my way through the last paragraph without screaming and am now feeling quite saintly. I would estimate that at least ninety per cent of those ✂ s had either facial hair or a hat. Now that I have delivered them all safely to their meeting rooms I can spend the rest of the morning behaving as though they no longer exist.)

ᕲ

We have so far run into two rather sticky stumbling blocks: the hero has absented himself, and the heroine (me) is having

12

a crisis about how much information she's prepared to part with. Sounds like it could get a bit tedious.

Do you believe in any of this? I wonder whether you think I'm making it up or not. My guess is that you don't, but for those of you that do, thank you for granting me those enchanting powers of invention.

What's the difference between imagining a story and finding yourself in one anyway? I was just thinking about a certain notorious serial killer and his exceptionally inventive existence – the jar of charred knickers, the crazed eugenic experiments, the public persona, the lies – and wondering why writerly invention has been so valourized. Is it because no one gets hurt (supposedly)? Why should acting out your ideas be deemed so inferior? (Unless you manage to do something so effective that other people have to write about you.) I'm not saying that I think this particular serial killer was a nice man or that he should be given a literary prize for having such a big imagination. I just mean that if he wrote it all down instead of doing it, people might think he was really great. Or even that if someone wrote a serious book about him, people might think it was really great. But, as it stands, most people don't think he is at all great (including me).

The reason all of this concerns me is that I feel it may tell me something I need to know. This guy had an extraordinary and terrible existence, and that's thought to be bad. Some people write books about extraordinary and terrible things, and that's thought to be good. Some people have lives where they never do anything extraordinary or terrible, and that's thought to be okay. And then here I am writing a book where nothing extraordinary or terrible will happen (as far as I know), and I fear this may make it awful. At first it seemed like a good idea, but now I'm not so sure. Can anything interesting come from a person who spends five days a week in an orthopaedic swivel chair? Perhaps I would be better off going out and doing something extraordinary (and not terrible) and leaving it to someone else to write about.

☎✕✕☎

I do think that active people are missing out, but when I start writing I feel a bit sad and stupid, like I'm doing a rather pathetic thing and should probably stop.

3

Love and Work

I'm in love and I have a job. These things make me very sad and very happy (they both do both). I don't know quite how they've got themselves so tangled up in my imaginary scheme of things, but right now the two seem inextricably linked in an intimate relation of extreme incompatibility. If I don't go to work I can't live so I can't be in love. If I do go to work I have to try to forget that I'm in love for long spells at a time. Because I'm in love I can't do my job properly – when I start feeling overly emotional it seems like an absolute outrage to me that there are other things I have to do.

I fall in love in a very unfortunate way. I really do all the wilting and swooning and waiting and going through all the more extravagant feelings in my sentiment-repertoire – plus new ones. This time I felt I was being electrocuted by my own electrons which, in my meagre experience, was quite unprecedented. All I could do in response was smoke, which made it a thousand times worse. When I'm in love I feel intolerably lively and when I'm at work I feel tragically close to death. I've got a kind of high-velocity Proserpina syndrome. If you have six months at a time in hell at least you have time to get used to it. You probably start to find ways to make the best of it. And then when you get back to your real life, at first it must feel like it's going to last for ever (like on the first day of a holiday). This daily double dose of lively and deathly ☎ ☎ ☎ ☎ ☎ ☎ ☎ is messing with my molecules and making me very, very agitated.

*　　*　　*

The Academy is an odd place. About a third of the people here are Doctors – all of whom appear to be passionately caught up with materials (and how they crack, deform, melt, mould and creep). The rest are doing things which have little in common with the preoccupations of the Doctors, but which wouldn't be there if the Doctors weren't there. They print things, post things, count things, move things from place to place and complain rather a lot. I suppose this sort of split makes it typical of most places ☎ where people go to work. The Doctors are distant and frequently display an air of embarrassment when they speak to you (some try to compensate for the difference in rank by being a bit too sweet). The paper/box/pen pushers are quick to become very familiar and are generally quite nice – except for when their contempt for the Doctors extends into a contempt for anyone who thinks that their life might be more pleasurably spent doing something other than pushing stuff ☎ ✎. My job feels a little different to all the other jobs in that I'm not a Doctor and I'm not strictly a pusher – most of the time I'm not actually doing anything. Which is how come I'm free to be doing this. Doing something like this is frowned on by Doctors and pushers alike, partly because it supposedly prevents you doing ☎ what you're meant to be doing (which, as I've said, is nearly nothing, which makes me wonder whether doing nothing visibly is part of the job – like the Queen) and partly because you're acting too much like you think you're a Doctor and that you might be capable of (enjoying) doing things that you've devised for yourself and are not entirely dependent on your superiors (for whom you feel only derision) to grant you a licence to exist.

4

The ᙭᙭᙭

When I try to write about romance everything goes wrong. I feel really blank and at a loss and it seems to have quite a lot to do with the love thing. It might be best to go back a bit and see how it started, and then perhaps it will become easier to talk about. ☎ The problem is that the character involved is the ᙭᙭᙭, so I'll only be able to tell you a fraction of the story. (This is insane. I really ought either to control my characters a bit better or make them up so they can't boss me around. (Although there are, I believe, instances of fictional characters taking on so much power that they start taking liberties with their own poor authors.)) Whatever, I'm going to have to tell you *something*. And perhaps, in the process, I'll find a way to figure out what on earth's going on. Hercule Poirot only needs about fifty per cent of the clues to piece together an entire murder.

When I first met the ᙭᙭᙭ I remember being rather under-impressed and trying constantly to find polite ways to terminate the conversation. I've heard this is how a number of the most stunning love affairs begin. It was in the street outside an art opening at the beginning of June. I was at my most indiscriminate and was being friendly to absolutely everyone. A friend introduced me to him and I remember finding him quite frightening. He had a kind of wild face and this scary way of looking at you that made you feel really *looked at*. He told me how difficult his life was and it seemed like he really meant it – although from what he was saying, his problems didn't seem so bad. Without meaning to be too indiscreet, it was all just institutional-type injustices and things that everybody has to deal with. But he appeared so intense when he talked about it that you almost had to believe he suffered it worse than anyone. People I've only just met are always telling me all the details of their lives (I definitely encourage it) but I wasn't really in the mood that day so, as soon as I got the chance, I excused myself and went in search of something more superficial. After that first meeting I didn't really remember him at all, and certainly not his name until, a few months later, I found myself borrowing a computer in a building where he was also doing some work. I started to bump into him as often as twice a day. Once he entrusted me with a broken camera while he went off to do some other things. Sometimes he'd run after me in the corridor, calling my name and asking for the time or for a cigarette (although I didn't used to smoke). Gradually I softened enough to surrender to the notion that he wasn't actively repellent – but nothing more. Or maybe a bit more, actually, because I remember calling him a pig one day for telling me I looked nice when I didn't. I guess I must have liked him a bit without noticing. He quickly pointed out that pigs can be charming and started to snort. It's ridiculous really, because when I picture him today he seems to me a paragon of masculine perfection. (Which makes me wonder which of the people I'm utterly indifferent to at the moment might turn into a person I can't take my mind off in the future. And, equally disturbing, how the AAAA himself might transform once more – within my understanding – into a wholly new type of creature.)

Feel free to skip:

All this is what goes on in a large percentage of classic romantic literature, isn't it? The indifference-to-love theme is a big one in Jane Austen, all the Brontës, Proust and almost everyone else dealing with passionate liasons. Is the reason it gets such good coverage something to do with the question of who knows what? It kind of flatters the onlooker who knows perfectly well that the two as yet unaffected characters are destined for each other. Narrative curiosity (have you noticed I've stopped putting the ☎s in quite so much? At the moment I hardly notice the phone) is aroused by the possibility that ☎ ✂ (now I've mentioned it it's started to get on my nerves again) they might be right about something or, more pleasurably, that they are having a profound insight into what goes on with other people. This, of course, is heavily aided by the tuition of the kindly author, who is prepared to supply all the leads in such a way as to make you imagine you're discovering things all by yourself. Obviously novels don't go like that so much these days (unless you like books with bold, gold lettering on the cover) but I can't work out whether that sort of detective/psychologist style writer-to-reader tuition may simply be out of my reach (I really don't understand people) ☎ or whether it's a rather retrograde approach and best left well alone. Perhaps these two options can be combined to form a third pose of being modish enough to claim that one can't fathom anyone or anything (particularly oneself) when secretly one feels that it might be quite helpful to understand things a little better. I'm afraid this one sounds most like me.

〜

After the three-month indifference period something rather ridiculous happened. At the end of the first week of September I stumbled across something which gave the whole game away in terms of his absolute excellence. (Now, 〰〰, do you regret your inadvertent ban on my circulating information about you? This bit could have shown you in such a good light.) This mysterious thing was enough to make me burst into tears on the spot. It was incontrovertible evidence of his passion, energy, wit, intelligence, sophistication, warmth and all-round brilliance etc. I sobbed all over him. It was one of my favourite cries ever. It couldn't have been more surprising. I was instantly and totally besotted (and ran away). I know this lack of detail must be very frustrating for you, so I'll try to tell you as much as I can about what happened without getting myself into trouble. It took place in a small, dark room in an institutional building. It showed quite clearly that his angst was a product of his extreme smartness and that he wasn't just an average moany guy. I tried to escape when I started blubbing, but he spotted me, all puffy and snivelling, and held out his arms for me to fall into them. It was delicious. He felt really amazing. I couldn't believe I was hugging and crying all over this person who I'd thought was pretty awful until I'd found myself calling him a pig in response to his implausible compliment. I might be friendly, but I'm really reserved and this isn't the sort of thing I normally do. I like to keep things a bit more under control. I was really enjoying the hug when suddenly I just got too embarrassed and had to break it off. I felt like, if I carried on hugging him, I didn't know where it would stop. I do kind of have a boyfriend – whom I'll tell you about later – but it wasn't only that. It was more that I freaked out because I had no idea what it all meant. I extracted myself from his arms, said something shamefully polite, and rushed outside.

After I left him was when I really started to get hung-up on how handsome and sexy he was. And, just in case that last bit left you feeling a little excluded, I might as well tell you what he looks like. I think it's entirely justified given the fact that he takes photographs. However thoroughly I do it, I'm sure you'd never recognize him in the street. He's not quite thirty years old. He has brown hair that stands up of its own accord. He has a very pronounced laughter line on his left cheek and permanent five o'clock shadow. His eyebrows meet in the middle, but he has long eyelashes to make up for it. He's about five foot ten and quite muscular. His hands are *huge*. He wears clothes that look like they might have been really smart until he started wearing them – like Yves St Laurent suits with holes in.

The next day I couldn't wait to bump into him. I had butterflies. I could hardly speak or eat. I was all over the place. But, perhaps because I was in such a ridiculous state, everyone seemed to want to talk to me. Nuns and nutters attached themselves to me in the street and, as usual, I didn't turn them away. People I'd met once came and told me their life histories. Long-estranged friends sought me out. Other friends wanted to go to tea. By the time I ran into the only person I had any strong desire to see I felt utterly emptied ☎ out. I wanted to collapse into his arms and kiss him ardently, but it was completely impossible. I could barely smile at him. We had a horrible little conversation and I wandered off feeling inconsolable. Overnight I had developed the idea that the ∿∿ was a person who could handle anything. Big feelings would be no problem. Tantrums would be a pleasure. If I exploded he'd look after the bits. At the back of my mind I suspected this was improbable, but I was still devastated by the banality of the meeting.

The next week was spent trying to invent a life for myself. At the same time as meeting the ∿∿ everything that had been keeping me going came to an end. I had just finished university. I had no job, no money, no plans and a terrifying feeling of lightness. Although I'm sure it isn't apparent, I'm over-educated enough, in all the wrong fields, to make finding an appropriate job nearly impossible. I actually took a Master's degree in the History of Punishment: from Ancient Greece to the Victorian Era. I've been advised to leave it off my CV in case potential employers find it off-putting. Which leaves my BA in Art History and a small handful of O and A Levels. This combination makes me pretty much useless to everyone. After five days of soul-searching in conditions of severe vexation, I decided to become a receptionist. Well, decided isn't exactly the word – I needed to pay the rent, and joining a temping agency was the only legal way I knew to make it possible.

I wasn't at all pleased about it. I used to temp during my university holidays and hated it so much that I had a metal bar stuck through my lip to wreck my face in such a way that I would never be able to get an office job again. Unfortunately, this metal bar is removable and only leaves a small hole in my skin.

Before putting this terrible job plan into action, I stayed up all night in a bar with a friend, agonizing. He has a Master's degree but works on a coffee stall and was very sympathetic. We agreed it was better to have crappy jobs and to keep doing the things we liked than to succumb to the temptations of a steady career. For nineteenth century types, who still believe in the figure of the genius/outcast, it seems preferable to do something that requires no wit or skill and pays no money than to do something that takes a bit of smartness and pays well. We attach a great deal of shame to remunerative professional activity. In retrospect I can see that this isn't necessarily very bright. But when I was drunk it made perfect sense to me. With encouragement from my friend, I decided that it would be a good idea to get the most boring job in London and read the whole of *Remembrance of Things Past*. It seemed better to me to be reading a book while doing something mindless than to be doing something interesting in itself and getting rich. (Although I now see that this logic has its flaws, I haven't found anything better to replace it with.)

I've heard there is a book about how reading Proust can affect your life. I wonder whether it talks about how it can make you become a receptionist.

The following Monday morning at nine o'clock – nine days after the crying incident – I received a call commanding me to appear at the Academy for a tryout. I pulled on my best blue suit and girl's shoes and hurried off to Piccadilly. I spent an entire seven hours feeling thoroughly ashamed of myself.

I couldn't believe I was having to do something so inane. I imagined that everyone who saw me would assume I was some sort of sorry lamebrain. I finished the day feeling wholly dejected, having earned thirty-six pounds. I felt it might be helpful to look at something interesting before going home, just to make sure interesting things still existed. I raced over to the nearest bit of art I could think of (I wasn't feeling at all discriminating) and bumped straight into the ∿∿∿. The 'bumping into' thing was one of the things that stopped when university and my belief in a rosy future stopped, so it surprises me now that I could have been so blasé about this particular instance of it. Looking back, it was something near a miracle. I said 'hi' rather jauntily, but I felt so foolish in my blue suit that I was in danger of launching into a profuse apology for it, my job, the hole in my face, and everything else that seemed to be wrong with the world. I thought it might be wise to cut the conversation short.

Luckily he didn't comply and followed me into the gallery. We went for coffees (for which I felt obliged to pay, in my new role as office-going breadwinner) and talked easily, seriously(ish) and nicely. After coffee we went to see more art and drank plastic cupfuls of very strong rum. He casually mentioned that he was going to leave the country in about three weeks' time and had already booked his ticket. It was hideous news. I didn't know quite how to take it. I was torn between trying to make something happen immediately – even if it was only a devastating fling – or running away before he made me too miserable.

At the exhibition there was a short film of an exploding plum, which you had to go into a small, dark box to see. When I got into the box with the ∿∿∿ I became really desperate to kiss him. I decided to give myself over completely to the temptations of an ill-fated love affair. However, since the first hug, which had happened so naturally, it had become impossible even to touch him. I thought if I kept watching the film and edged up to him a bit, he might get the hint, but he didn't. It was awful. Still, we chatted and laughed about the stuff in the exhibition, which mostly really stank, and I found myself liking him more and more.

After the show we were taken out for a Chinese meal by a very earnest friend of his, and finally went off on our own for more coffees in Soho. I was so pleased to be with him and it felt so right that it didn't really strike me how likely it was that I might never see him again. I no longer had access to the computer I'd been borrowing and he had stopped working in that building anyway. Our chance meeting in the gallery was a fluke unlikely to repeat itself in the twenty-one days before his plane was due to depart. London can seem like a sickeningly huge place sometimes.

For some reason I felt incapable of doing anything to make another meeting certain. I couldn't even ask for his number. On the way back to the tube I gave him a book that I happened to be carrying (and which I was sure he wouldn't read) and then kissed him rather stiffly on the cheek before scuttling down the stairs at the entrance to Leicester Square station.

Disaster struck. I approached the ticket machines feeling like the whole of everything had been taken away and replaced by a very inferior version. Nothing had any substance any more. My body felt like a skinful of low-density gas. I didn't know whether I would pass out or keep going – and I couldn't think which alternative was better. It was all most unexpected.

When I was very young I had a toy theatre with a thin metal stage floor. The little wooden characters (a royal family and courtiers) had magnets where their feet might have been. There was a pair of magnetized sticks that you were meant to insert under the stage floor so that the figures could be moved around without being touched. Well, the point of all this is that, when I said goodby and sloped off, I felt like one of those figures. It was like someone else was deciding what I should do. I knew exactly what I wanted to happen (instantaneous breakdown of all psychic and physical distance resulting in violent orgasms, followed by cigarettes) but some very powerful force seemed to be preventing me from even trying to bring it about. Imagining the texture of his skin and all the details of intimacy was so easy when he was there drinking coffee that it seemed clumsy to push anything. But as soon as we'd said goodbye all my daydreams were punctured by the fact that he was gone, and there was no longer any chance of them coming true.

The sensations I suffered as I crossed the station felt like a fusion of whatever was going on now with every disappointment and disappearance (including the happy birthday one) in my entire history. It didn't feel like I'd just failed to kiss a man (whatever that feels like, if not this). It felt more like I'd let the entire planet slip off its axis and spin into obscurity. I'm an absurd character. Every time I say goodbye, even on a good day, I feel like something terrible has happened. At the very best I'm crushed by an irrepressible feeling of doom. This time it was multiplied by a thousand because the person I had said goodbye to was someone I had accidentally fallen completely in love with and who was about to leave England for good. It really seemed to me like I might have fucked up my whole life forever.

Anyhow, drama, catastrophe, ruination, etc. When I arrived at the top of the escalator, who should be just ahead of me, but the ᗯᗯ? In my insistence on saying goodbye against my will, it had never occurred to me to check whether or not he was getting the tube home too. We took the escalator down together, standing very close but, given the rather extreme circumstances, I was still finding it impossible to make anything happen. When we reached the bottom, if I didn't act quickly, we would fork off toward our separate trains and my guts (which had thankfully landed back in my skin) would be forced to re-evacuate.

Happily, my inertia prevented me from making any verbal declarations. My inactivity paid off. When we got to the bottom of the escalator it started to happen properly like it does in stories. We turned and faced each other and stared straight into each other's eyes. It was excellent. We were just looking, but at last it felt like something was happening.

〜

Things are happening all the time, but sometimes you can feel it and sometimes you can't. It's got nothing much to do with the things themselves and everything to do with you. Obvious or what? But these small, important facts can still sometimes take me by surprise.☎

(Just as I'm writing this now, the 〰〰 himself rings me up – things have come a long way since the tube episode, although it was only about six weeks ago and because I have this flashy new receptionist's headset and am still confused about what I'm doing with my hands, I cut him off.)[1]

〜

We kissed. Next came all the pragmatic problems of what to do and where to go – all of which were awkwardly solved by the fact

[1] Have you noticed that the ☎s are greatly reduced? It's because the new headset leaves my hands freer to write (and cut people off) which means I don't feel quite so distracted by the phone. I'm virtually unimpeded by the fact that I have a job. And now I can be in love as much as I like. Whooppee!

Do you mind the odd footnote? It's quite good down here. Up there it feels like I'm talking out loud, while down here it's more like I'm whispering in your ear. Andy Warhol said he preferred to talk to his friends on the phone because the voice going straight into the ear felt more intimate. Proust found the same thing the first time he rang his grandmother. Maybe we could say that up there is like a letter and down here is more like a phone call (also because of the way footnotes burst in at random moments).

that he couldn't come to my house due to the presence of my boyfriend. This unfortunate fact tumbled out in a really dumb conversation where I told him I didn't want to do anything 'unethical' and he offered to sleep on the floor. We eventually decided to take the tube to his house, and kissed all the way. I really love kissing, but I'm pretty fussy about how it's done. I like wet, muscular kisses mixed with bites. I like kissing to be chaotic and messy and a bit like fighting. I hate soppy kisses (unless they're sandwiched between the other sort). Nobody much seems to kiss in the way that I like, and I hate to frighten people by trying it on them anyway. The whole point is that they have to do it of their own accord. So one of the best things about the MMM is that he just happens to kiss in the best possible way – which I could never have known until it happened.

When we got to his tube stop all this perfection was momentarily marred by a female voice calling out his name. He tried to duck into an exit, but she caught up with us anyway. When you don't really know someone their friends seem so terrifying. This girl really worried me. Why was he trying to hide? There seemed to be no escape from her so we all walked home together – and, to be fair, she was quite nice. His house was a bit of a surprise though. It was a crumbly nineteen-thirties thing, only just about fit for human habitation. There were about ten other people living there and none of them were particularly good friends. Just to make it doubly depressing they were also due to be kicked out before the end of the week.

Because there was no living room and the kitchen was completely revolting, we went straight to his room. I came over all shy and tongue-tied, but for once I almost enjoyed it. Sometimes shyness can be a pain in the arse, but occasionally you can really get into it. At odd moments I can see that it's quite appropriate and might almost be endearing. In the past I have gone to bed with a few more people than is strictly necessary, so it was nice to meet someone really spectacular and find myself behaving innocently.

After tea and tentative talk we went to bed. Something about it seemed uncannily 'right' again (despite the fact that he didn't have sheets, just a bundle of aeroplane blankets). So right, in fact, that it felt too ordinary. All the shyness and oddness dissipated and I felt pathetically flat. It's something a lot of people talk about. Your wishes turn boring on you when they actually begin to be granted. The things you have spent so long dreaming about aren't nearly so thrilling when you find yourself actually doing them. I know that some say they find this very disappointing and take it as a cue to leave, but my expectations were so high I wasn't prepared to give up on them yet. (I'm a heroine after all, and it would be irresponsible to desert my hero before anything had happened.)

Happily, something intervened. Neither of us had any condoms. It was great. This stupid thing that we thought we were going to do, we weren't. It's amazing what effect a tiny change of plan can have on your feelings. One minor frustration and the infatuation was back. We did all the stuff you do when you don't have sex (well, some of it). And suddenly I LOVED being in bed with him. It was fantastic. He didn't even have to try – I was just climaxing all over the place. It was partly to do with him – I couldn't have felt like that without him there – but he didn't have to do anything (technical) to make me have yet another orgasm. It was him, but it wasn't what he did. It was outside him and beyond him, but he had to be there too. I'm on the verge of sounding religious. I'll shut up.

As if that wasn't enough he also sang some of my favourite songs in a really beautiful soft voice and stroked me and cuddled me and kissed me for hours. I badly wanted to tell him that the things he was making me feel were better than all the other feelings I had had before, but it seemed too corny to say it, so I didn't.

At about four o'clock in the morning I realized I'd better get

28

going. I had a boyfriend and an early morning appointment. I got careless. Of course I'd see him again. I felt so *with* him I couldn't conceive of being completely without him. We went to the bus stop and I almost leaped on the night bus without giving him my number. But then he asked for it, which was a big relief. He'd ring me up. The world wasn't going to have to vaporize the minute the doors closed behind me.

I realize now though that the clumsy way in which I left him may have been almost entirely to blame for the bit that happened next.

(I hope I haven't overstepped the mark with the information I have just given, but I'm sure even his mother wouldn't spot him if she read it.)

⌒

I went home and did the things I had to do. My boyfriend and I were redecorating. If we couldn't agree on a colour we'd go for white (which is a big clue to the kind of relationship we have).

I know it's probably not smart to share a bedroom with someone you are not exactly in love with, but this is what I am doing. I'm doing it for a number of complex reasons, some of which I know, but many of which I probably don't. One of the big reasons is that my boyfriend and I rent a beautiful flat and would hate to lose it. It sounds pathetic, but if you could see our home you'd know what I meant. It's massive, with high ceilings and lots of light. It has a huge archway in the hall and amazing mouldings. The living room is the size of half a tennis court. It's right in the centre of town but, thanks to some bizarre idiosyncracy on the part of the landlord, it costs about the same as the average studio flat in Stockwell. If one of us leaves, despite its cheapness the other won't be able to afford to live here. It would seem almost immoral to let it go. Another reason for not separating is that we have been together for a number of years and find it difficult to imagine being apart. Although we're not overtly in love we really do like each other.

I don't think I really wanted to deal with this delicate problem, but now I have met someone else I may have to. I don't know whether I'm upset or relieved. I can't go on living in this stupid way, but I don't know what to do about it. The most Machiavellian solution would be for me to persuade the new lover to move in the day the boyfriend moves out. I don't think this would work. We might turn out not to like each other. I'd be faced with the same problem all over again. Not to mention the fact that the Λ/V/V is absolutely penniless and probably wouldn't be able to pay half of the rent. The flat is more mine than my boyfriend's (I lived there first) and I can't offer to move out and leave it to him anyhow, as he wouldn't be able to afford it on his own. Maybe he will meet someone else and I can perform this noble gesture.

~

During the first few days following my night with the Λ/V/V I was left on my own at home (the job was yet to begin officially), whitewashing. I imagined the Λ/V/V would leave it a few days before calling, so it took me a while to register how much I wanted him to. On the fourth day I decided he'd ring. It was horrible. Waiting for the phone is one of the most repulsive ways to pass time. When someone isn't calling, you just can't know what they're doing. If you start imagining what they might be up to, the possibilities (which all cruelly exclude you) go on for ever, involving infinite variations on themes, all of which you'd hate to be the case: that he's secretly married, that he's already left the country, that he picks up gorgeous girls every time he goes out (sometimes he doesn't even go out, he just beckons from his window), that he's a wealthy playboy, that he's a vile and heartless seducer, that he despises all sentiment, that he doesn't want you around in the slightest. Or, maybe equally disconcerting, that he's sad and lonely and pathetic and desperate to call but doesn't dare. I supposed they were all possible, but the first lot were the scenes I really dwelled on. I don't remember ever being quite so keen to be rung. After what seemed to me to have been such a perfect night, I couldn't understand what was keeping him away. I supposed I'd been quite gauche about the whole thing – like rushing off and nearly not leaving my number. It seemed possible that he thought I didn't like him too much. I know sometimes that can be a good thing (there's nothing more compromising than letting someone you hardly know in on the fact that you're completely obsessed with them) – but this time I felt that it wasn't.

I think I selected, from the limitless catalogue of possibilities, the notion that he'd decided I was attached and therefore a bad bet, and had gone out and seduced someone else the very next night. It was unspeakable. I went berserk. I stopped eating and sleeping and couldn't let it drop. (I also started writing in notebooks – something I had never done before in my life.) It seemed hopeless. His house had already been evacuated. I had no idea where he might be or how to reach him. I thought he wasn't ringing because of a misunderstanding brought about by my backwardness. Maybe I'm a bit arrogant in that way. Only I don't think so. It was just the last hopeful thought I could muster. Not calling is wicked and people should think hard before they do it. The only upside of not calling is that, for something that consists of absolutely nothing – no action, no substance, no anything – it has very extreme effects: it's fantastically economical. The downside is that these effects are insufferable. One of the worst results of not being called is that music becomes excessively meaningful. While I was waiting to be telephoned I listened to Beethoven's eleventh piano sonata over and over again. I didn't even enjoy it – it made me feel sick. I believe Beethoven suffered a serious episode of unrequited love.

31

You can hear it listening to this sonata. I think it comes across in the endlessly repeating, distorting phrases and the modulating harmonies. It's a musical equivalent of the ceaseless internal discussions you have when you're obsessively infatuated. You can't completely change the topic, so you just try to find as many variations on it as you can. You have beautiful and soothing bits (when you actually believe that the other person likes you and is just about to ring), monstrous and hard-to-listen-to bits (when you don't), lulls and crescendos. The only difference is that the sonata is only about twenty minutes long – meaning that you have to play it over and over again.

Seven days after staying with the ⋀⋀⋀ I went to work full-time at the Academy. To coincide with starting my new job, I began to have panic attacks every day at two o'clock. I was stranded at my switchboard not knowing what on earth was going on. I'd hold my hand over the receiver deciding whether or not to get someone to come and rescue me. I felt like a fucking nutcase. All I could think about were the unbelievably minor things I might have to do (answer the phone, act like a girl, stay in my chair, pee, and cycle home) and how it was going to be utterly impossible to do any of them. I don't know what I imagined might go wrong, but I felt as if any sort of exertion (which included sitting still) might cause me to die or fall into a coma or start ranting unstoppably (the worst). I can't quite see why now, but at the time it was all very real. The only way to stop it was to lose consciousness for about ten seconds, after which I would transform into a perfectly sensible young lady. I just had to shut my eyes and hope to pass out before the telephone rang. It was hardly an ideal way to begin my reception career, spending the first part of each afternoon trying to conk out.

The only other thing that could snap me out of my panics was a long string of abuse – interspersed with the word 'darlin' – delivered by the Academy's ex-receptionist, who still works here (and whom you will meet properly in the next chapter).

If I couldn't get any sleep, I knew I could call him on the phone to ask for some small favour and be told to fuck off in a fantastic variety of brutal ways. Something about his baroque rudeness would make me instantly better. I think I just needed someone to relate to, and the only person I felt understood by was someone who could acknowledge how profoundly worthless I was. If I rang and asked for some headed notepaper he would tell me that I was a graceless, ugly bitch with no redeeming features, who might as well go and die in a pit. I would recover at once.

I started to become acutely overwrought about the switchboard after I left my work number on my home ansaphone. When I was at home, if the phone rang I'd go nuts. My heart, head, limbs and voice would all go erratic on me until I'd ascertained that it wasn't him and could fall back into a subdued version of normal. At home it would happen about five times a night, but at work it was more frequent. Every beep the switchboard made would set me off. Countless times a day my body would have to do its freaky things. Phone call after phone call after phone call would trigger all my symptoms. I was like a mechanical toy with an over-enthusiastic owner. I was never allowed to wind down before the next bout of spasms.

At night, when I couldn't sleep, I would read *A Lover's Discourse* (the nearest thing to self-help I'll allow myself). It was dreadful. It talks about the phone a lot, but technology has changed since Roland Barthes's day. He couldn't have had a clue how things might go, so it's hardly his fault, but his problems weren't my problems and I hated him for it. It's so horrible when you try to find a point of empathy in the world and the only one you can think of fails you. He rabbits on about not being able to go to the toilet or the shop in case the desperately awaited phone call comes and he misses it. I have an ansaphone for that. And 1471. And he goes on about not being able to talk on the phone in case the object of his crush

33

tries to ring and finds him engaged. I have a 'call waiting' service on my line. He talks about these obstructions as if they're bad. They're not. They're good. At least he could have a fantasy that the person had tried to call and failed and that they loved him and were disappointed. I knew for an undeniable fact that the ∧∧∧ had made absolutely no fucking attempt whatsoever to ring me. I hate advanced communication technology with its dumb pretence that it removes the impediments that occasionally make contact difficult. What about the difficulties that come when the person you're waiting around for might not actually like you? At moments like this it would really help to have a crappy phone system to bitch about.

∽

I know I'm spoiling the story but I just have to break off to rant about the ∧∧∧. I can't go on writing about how much I like him at a moment when he's making me so furious. All this mooning around is old news. Everything he does now seems perfectly gauged to annoy. Friends tell me he's terrible. I still adore him partly, but hate him too. He rushes about in such a pain in the arse way. He's sub-human. He's a freak. He's the most impossible person to relate to. It's as if the blinds have gone down in his brain. He is developing a permanently glazed, maniacal look as if he is gradually blotting out the reality of other human beings. He's always ranting about some new scheme. The last time we spoke he said he wanted to make a walking billboard and take it round the world. Before that it was gadgets for girls to pee standing up. Then there were toys for urinals that he said would make him a millionaire. What happened to the ∧∧∧ I fell in love with? He screams in the street for no reason and then apologizes to passers-by. I really am breaking the rules by telling you this, but I sometimes think the guy is going nuts. Why should I care about protecting him anyway when he's so careless with me? What have I done to

34

deserve this? He's so charming and then so hideous and mean. I keep evenings aside at his request and then he fucks them up. I have to re-invite him – I think he pretends he's forgotten – and then he gets all belligerent. 'What have you got planned?' he asks. 'Why are you pestering me? . . . What do you want?' (Which, admittedly, is a question worth asking.) He makes me feel terrible. But the most annoying thing is that he makes me feel so intolerably crap that I have to put in some really intensive intellectual and emotional labour to cure myself to a point where I almost don't feel bad any more, and then the next time I speak to him I've forgotten how cruel he is and don't prepare myself against his malice. How can I go on talking about love when I detest him so thoroughly? (It could all change in a minute if he calls.)

I can't believe I'm at work again waiting for him to ring. This time there are no palpitations, just a confused feeling of rage. He's going to give me cancer. (But I hate nice boys.)

～

It's a really particular skill to set up indecipherable situations, or to perform impenetrable actions, and then to leave. The ⋁⋀⋁⋀ has this skill and displayed his virtuosity to me this morning at the Academy. Sudden departures, in any case, aren't really my bag. But in conjunction with the unintelligible performances they really knock me off balance. Today he came to the Academy in full cycle courier gear to say that he had decided to stay in the country, after which he jumped on my desk and took a picture of me, and then got really irritable when I asked if he'd like to meet up later. (He left saying he'd call, though. But so far he hasn't.)

～

Fuck. I've got to go home in twelve minutes and he hasn't

rung. I don't think he will. Maybe he'll call me at ☎☎ my flat. Maybe he'll go to the café I suggested. ☎☎☎ I think not. Would I stoop to calling him? (No way.) It's quite good being this shaken up – but I don't think I should thank him. This particular pleasure is auto-romantic – he just helps to exacerbate it. No phone call yet (six minutes to go). ☎ I feel really sexy. ☎☎ How infuriating. What am I getting out of all this? Why aren't I happy ☎ with my nice, ☎ sweet boyfriend? I've got to sort ✄ ✄ myself out. I'll fall in love with my analyst (although I haven't seen him for a couple of years). I'll fall in love with anyone. I don't ☎ care. Two ☎ minutes ☎. I'll fall in love with myself (I can feel it happening already). I'm a bit happier. ☎ Time's up and no call. Fuck. (I always get the most phonecalls right at the end of the day.)

∽

Now I'm in the café where I suggested we meet. He had no idea where it was so he won't show. But I've got it badly enough to sit here for half an hour anyway. I'll look up when the door opens like I actually think he's coming. Fuck him. Fuck everything. Fuck myself. I'm a fucking idiot. I just went to the National Gallery to look at pictures of people being eaten by dragons. I feel like dragonfood myself right now. I'd just hand myself over without a fight -- chuck myself in its mouth even if it wasn't hungry. I could do with a bit of piercing with arrows too. I don't care if it's histrionic. My head's spinning and I feel nauseous. Now I feel like going home, although I don't feel like seeing my boyfriend. I'll have one more cigarette and disappear (I wish). Maybe I'll crash on the way back. But I never really think I'll crash when I'm wearing all black. It's too untheatrical. If I wear pale things all I can think about is getting run over. (Remember Moira Shearer's blood-stained white tights at the end of *The Red Shoes*?) Today a crash would be so unphotogenic that I might as well just get home in one piece and suffer the consequences. I hope I never thank him for what he's putting me through, but my guess is that I will. Or I'll wake up rational and realize I bring it on myself.

I ought to be able to transform my misery into something else through writing, but instead I just write about it and it stays the same.

I'll go before I get tongue cancer from smoking too many filterless cigarettes. It sounds gruesome. I've never written so much in my life. I think I only feel like writing when things are going astray. But I might not be able to write any more anyhow if I lose my job – which looks possible after today. I really messed up and took too many liberties and everyone got cross. I'm destitute.

I can't bear to go home and face all my problems there either. My boyfriend and I have been doing a very good job of avoiding discussing what's happening. But I don't think I can put on any sort of show for him right now. I can't go home and cook and chat about my day. I feel like going foetal and hiding under the dining table. He knows about the MMM; but I'm afraid that if I tell him the real extent of my feelings I will mess up both of our lives. What are we going to do with our home and with each other? How have I got myself caught up in this stupid situation?

⌐

I just went back to work to pick my bike up and the night porter told me the MMM had rung. I called back and now I'm on my way to see him. I'm happy. How things turn around.

This whole romance is doomed, isn't it? I know I haven't told you much about the MMM but it occurs to me that right now you might be in much the same position as the reader of classic fiction: you probably have some very good ideas about what's going on and where it could be leading. Maybe you can see quite clearly what will happen to me. I wish you could tell me. I feel utterly clueless. I suppose the options are, briefly: a long/short miserable/happy affair, a long/short miserable/happy marriage, death or disappearance of one or both of us and that's about it.

Do you really care what happens? I imagine not, but I'd still love to hear what you thought was going on. It's just a little unfortunate that by the time you come to read this you won't be able to help much – as presumably I'll have reached some sort of conclusion already.

5

Slice

As the receptionist I see very little of what happens at the Academy. I have no idea where people sit, what their work involves or what their offices look like. While I may spend each day in this building, ostensibly doing something that seriously affects all the other people in it, I have very little to say about the institution itself. I'm stuck down ✂ by the door, putting anonymous callers through to people I hardly know so that they can talk about things I don't care about. I have worked as a temporary receptionist before and I know that it makes no difference whether the calls I transfer are concerned with the discussion of engineering materials, pop music, underwear, petrol or serious fraud. (The only difference I have ever noticed is that if the calls are concerning advertising then the people around me are a self-important bunch of bastards.) All I do is connect a name with an extension number, pass the caller on as quickly as possible and get back to my own business. While I may have a vague interest in sophisticated new materials ✂ ✂ (I just read a long article about a plastic that behaves exactly like wood, but which doesn't warp or rot) I definitely don't care how the Academy pays its bills, organizes its conferences, edits its journals or selects its members. The callers often fail to understand this, and sometimes even refer to the Academy as mine. The Academy is not mine, it's someone else's. I think it may even belong to the Queen. When people ring up and ask me when my Annual Dinner is, what my postcode is, what date my next publication is due out, or when my chief consultant is back from his holidays, I don't know what to say. I don't have an Annual Dinner. Why on earth would a complete stranger want my postcode? My next publication is supposed to be this one, but it might never come out. My chief consultant is my best friend and she's not on holiday. It makes me very angry. It reminds me how annoyed I am about being here and being treated like this is my sole purpose in life. I am not a receptionist. I am someone who comes and behaves like a receptionist in a randomly selected company that I don't give a toss about. What I guess I'm secretly trying to say here is that, while I'm about to attempt to describe the office, you'll have to take it with a dash of scepticism because I don't actually know too much about it. ☎☎ I just feel I should tell you vaguely who's here and what they're like in case it becomes relevant later. I can't stand it when people talk about their friends and colleagues as if you know who they are when you don't. At least if you have some loose picture of who I work with and where each one fits in relation to the others, then I will be able to bitch and gossip about them with a little less fear of sending you to sleep.

At the top of the office pecking order we have Professor X., whose speech is so unfeasibly posh it's ceased to sound like English and has transformed itself into an agonized assortment of drawn-out vowels (perhaps twice as many as his more lowly compatriots), accentuated by crackling noises and showers of spit. He's so ridiculous it's cheap to ridicule him. He gets his tea first and all his calls are vetted by his nineteen-fifties spinster-style secretary/translator – carefully chosen for her cringing fearfulness and unshakeable devotion. If she was fictional you'd have every reason to be disappointed in the writer for inserting such a trite and familiar character. The only things about her that extend beyond the representations of secretaries in dodgy films and novels are her constant – and always seemingly polite – lavatorial references. She's always telling people in the corridor about inconvenient moments at which she's had to pee and

40

which drinks go straight through her and how she can open the door to her office with her bum.

At the bottom of the stack (even below me, if I was ever petty enough to pull rank) is Heck. Heck is amazing. He really hates to work, and what he counts as work is very little. Moving an envelope two inches would be counted as work by Heck. Sitting in the same room as a box counts as work to Heck. Heck shouted at me for a full minute (using up all that was left of his meagre energy supply) when I ✍ once caused a box to appear in his room. He warned me that sitting near a box was more than he could cope with. All he had to do was ignore it until its owner came and took it away, but it exhausted him. He can do resentment very brilliantly but, unhappily for him, no one seems to appreciate his excellence in the field because he comes from a country of which laziness is thought by certain English people to be a national attribute. They put his fantastic lethargy and umbrage down to mere cultural heredity and don't give him his due. It's as if his singular brand of torpid malice comes from something so much bigger than him and his particular existence that they can't even begin to contemplate it without risking being swamped by a vast confusion. I try to allow myself to reflect upon him but, quite frankly, I can't either. Heck traumatizes me. His rancour gives me vertigo. When he's lazy and grouchy it seems to be half to do with him and half to do with the history of the world. His problems are gargantuan. He's impossible. He had to move some objects yesterday and is threatening ☎✂ to take tomorrow off to nurse his injuries.

I just stopped writing for nearly two hours. All I felt like doing was sitting still and staring. Writing suddenly seems very difficult just because you bump into things that you feel you have to include but that you don't feel capable of dealing with (like Heck). Heck got me really stuck but, rather than oust him altogether, I think he should stand as testament to my unfortunate limitations.

* * *

In between the very top and the very bottom, are all sorts of seemingly unrelated people performing seemingly unrelated tasks. However, they are all clearly related somehow or the office would collapse. Quite a few of them are related to one another by marriage too – a fact which I find surprising. What must it be like to have a spouse and a job all in the same place at the same time?

Alongside Heck we have an old geezer whose job description is unclear – to him as well as to others. Because of this he makes it his business to interfere with everyone else's work and to tell them how better to go about it. ☎ ☎ He's married to someone in the accounts department. I imagine it's because she is so effective that they have invited her dismal husband to come and sit in the cellar and pretend to have a job. Perhaps they allow it because she's a nice lady and has worked for the Academy for a very long time. Most companies probably wouldn't employ people in this strange, philanthropic way, but this place has an old fashioned, family feel and does stuff that more ☎✂☎ cut-throat businesses wouldn't. The old geezer seems to be well aware of this set-up, which is why he loves to tell stories about how much he bosses his wife around at home. She brings him a packed lunch every day, which she leaves on my desk for him to collect.

He hates young people and is always keen to tell the office manager about the terrible things we have done. He clearly hopes that he will be able to get rid of one of us, steal our job and give himself a legitimate reason for being here. Sadly for him, though, no one really has it in them to do anything particularly naughty, so he never has any good stories to tell. He could, of course, make up them up, but he doesn't have the wit.

(I try hard never to be naughty as I need to keep this job or else I might be forced to get one where I am required to perform time-consuming tasks. Despite the fact that I hate it, I am genuinely trying to be a ☎ perfect receptionist. Unfortunately

I believe I am very far from succeeding.)

The office manager is my main enemy at the Academy. She tries to be my boss. She is a stocky, Enid Blyton-style headmistress character who is quite unaware of how wild her taste in clothes appears to everyone else. She loves zig-zags and flower patterns teamed with checks and spots in reds, lilacs and tangerines. She frowns on eccentricities in other people but is blissfully unaware of the fact that she dresses like a crazy person. If I wore her clothes I would be fired at once. It would be impossible not to think she was blind if she didn't have such a good eye for small coffee droplets on floor tiles and thumbprints on brass doornobs, both of which make her froth ✂ at the mouth. She isn't related to anyone by marriage, and only just about passes for someone related to other human beings by blood. She has a super-human temper. I hate her. She loves to talk to me like I know ☎✂ nothing about anything. She has no idea who I am. She has never asked me a question that involves anything other than inquiring as to whether or not I've done something yet.

She's not even good at her job. The office manager is hardly ever where she should be because she's always somewhere else, blaming someone else for her previous fuck-up. It takes her so much time to tell them off that she ends up getting behind on her bollockings. Sometimes you have to sit through a tantrum relating to the fuck-up she made a week earlier. Every so often she lags so far behind on her blameful rages that she can no longer even pretend to relate them to real events – the disasters themselves ☎ having receded so far into the past ☎ that nobody has retained even the vaguest memory of what they might have been. At this point she falls silent for a day or two, simply allowing everyone to feel how much she despises them, and then starts again from scratch.

She never picks up her telephone, so all her angry callers end up yelling at me because I'm as near as they're ever ☎☎☎ going to get to her. ✍ The most effective strategy I have come up with for dealing with this problem is to take their side and

43

agree that the office manager is useless and terrible. They are so surprised by my lack of company loyalty that they feel sorry for the Academy and quit whining at once.

The office manager has a helper who detests her with an impressively violent passion, but who will probably never leave her as I'm sure he secretly fears his entire character would disintegrate if it lost its defining hate-object. Without the office manager to loathe he might only be a quarter of what he is now. I like to believe that, after a few weeks without her, he might be surprised to find the missing three-quarters growing back in new, improved form. He came to work here when he was an eighteen-year-old reprobate and is now a thirty-year-old man with kids. He reads the jobs section of the paper every day but never makes any applications. He says he'd like to be a fireman, which seems to me like a brilliant idea, but he never does anything about it. Maybe he is afraid of being burned and leaving his children to starve. Maybe his wife is afraid of this too. Or maybe he uses his wife and children to justify his own timidity. Why doesn't he think of alternative jobs that are slightly less dangerous? I'm sure he will remain at the Academy until he becomes a granddad.

Next are the printers. They are confined to a tiny room taken up mostly by the big machines that churn out all the invites and information slips distributed by the Academy. I have to maintain as good a relationship as possible with these people as they are the ones elected to free me if I ever need to go to the toilet.

One of the cruellest aspects of the receptionist's job is that you are not free to leave the desk to go to the bathroom. If you wander off for as little as three minutes all sorts of things can go wrong. The President (who works from home) might call and get no reply and believe that all his staff have ganged up and taken a holiday without telling him. Members might ring, ☎✂☎ imagine the Academy has secretly moved to a new

44

address, feel betrayed and cease to pay their subscription fees. Or a lunatic might walk through the front door and massacre all the people in the office. (If I was at the desk I would, of course, be able to persuade him not to do this.)

The printers are perfectly nice people, but this peeing thing puts quite a strain on our friendship. I hate having to negotiate with them every time I want to use the bathroom. They're so uncool about it. They're always telling me that they're too busy, that they'll be free in fifteen minutes, or that they'll be here right away (which is a lie designed to shut me up). It feels very undignified to have to beg these people to allow me to go to the toilet. Sometimes they make me wait so long that, by the time I'm allowed to go, I've forgotten that I ever wanted to in the first place. I've crossed my legs for such ☎ a long time that I realize I can delay my pee for ever. I end up pretending to go to the toilet because, after hassling them so ferociously, I don't want them to believe it was all for nothing.[1]

If I was a man and could pee in the discreet standing position, I would certainly piss all over the horrible corporate vegetation that loiters uselessly around my desk. Perhaps this is something I could chat with the stuffy secretary about.

Slightly above the printers are the computer people. The first is a nice boy who probably doesn't like computers very much, but is capable of understanding them and needs an average job that pays an average amount of money to pay for his average flat, average food consumption, average bills, average friends' birthday presents, and average rounds of drinks. I'm sure he's as much of a freak as anyone else, but I have neither the time nor the inclination to find out why.

---

[1] One of the two people I've ever been passionately in love with in my entire life just rang me up to say that he'd met someone else, but that he'd forgotten her name so he was too embarrassed to call her. I'm surprised at how disgruntled I feel.

The second computer person is a friendly, chubby man with a moustache. He must be called Dave and is one of the most popular people in the office because of the way he knows how to make rude jokes which don't offend anyone. This seems to be the kind of joke that people in offices like, but is also the kind of joke that you forget immediately afterwards ☎ so, although ☎ I rack my brains, I can't come up with a single example. I think it isn't the content of the joke that counts, but the fact that it does this thing of being crude at the same time as not being. He is married to one of the prettiest girls at the Academy.

The third computer person is my favourite. He's so archetypally and essentially a computer fiend that you can't believe he has come down to earth to mix with the other atypical, slightly mixed up IT people, who mostly give the impression that they could be doing something else. Whatever he did, people would always know that he was fundamentally a friend of computers. His flesh is pulpy and muscle-free. He has thick glasses and his hair is sticky and full of flakes. I am embarrassed to describe him as I can't tell whether I am cruelly stereotyping him or whether he's already done it to himself.

I like him much more than the cliché secretary, though, so I'll try to do him again in a more generous and humanizing way:

The third computer person is a kind man with rounded features. He comes in late and wears a blue mac. He helps me when my computer breaks down, which makes me feel well-disposed towards him, but I find him hard to converse with. He laughs if I try to make a joke, but doesn't ever quite manage to join in and make one back. Joking is the only form of conversation I can imagine having with him as I am afraid that if we ever talked seriously I'd be forced to acknowledge his unbearable pain.

I don't know how I feel about this second effort. Is it any less cruel and insulting than the first? I don't know. But, instead of having some dull crisis about the violent inadequacy of language (or, worse, my own violently inadequate use of it) I'll try to remember that I don't have a hope in hell of describing these people a hundred per cent accurately and just get on with being partial. While I'm sure they are all worthy protagonists of their own stories, they are no more than bit-parts in mine. If I start thinking too hard about the complex psyches of all the people whose calls I connect it might cause me to have a breakdown. If I keep them flat and cartoon-like I can just about do my job and continue to negotiate my own existence.

Further up (a little less than halfway, I'd say) are the accounts and membership departments. The accounts people ☎✂☎✂☎ are a mixture of young and old, men and women, and are, with one striking exception, monstrously ugly. The one beautiful girl in accounts is the most unhappy person I have ever met. Her monstrous colleagues make her life hell. Unfortunately, sadness seems to suit her. The more her hideous workmates torment her and make her suffer, the more devastatingly attractive she becomes. The more her eyes fill up with angst and her mouth turns down at the corners, the more her beauty touches you and makes you fall in love with her. If they could just learn to be nice to her, she might turn into an ordinarily pretty girl.

What ugly people don't seem to understand is that being beautiful isn't necessarily an advantage. While physical beauty may mean that a person with no skills whatsoever can still get rich by marrying someone, this sort of trick is far from guaranteed to make a pretty person happy. Pretty people are often desperate to prove that this isn't their game and that, in fact, they have as many useful skills as the uglies and are equally keen to use them. While the uglies feel that, having been born so vile looking, they must learn some very good strategies to make sure they are accepted and valued by the rest of the world (they learn to tell jokes well, to be kind, to understand the magnetic laws governing the universe, to do

47

magic tricks, etc.) the beauties have to overcome the obstacles placed in front of them by the uglies, who want to believe that people with desirable faces and bodies have no talent due to the fact that they have been born without spots, droopy chins or snivelling dog-noses. In the end it might be fairest to say that the beauties really do have an advantage, but largely because the uglies give it to them. The beauties end up being faced with as many character-building obstacles as the uglies but, on overcoming them, are not only characterful but beautiful too. If the ugly people want to get ahead they should certainly get used to being nicer to the beautiful people for purely tactical reasons. Maybe without the incentives given by the uglies, the beauties really would just hang about and get money ☎ in return for being pretty and leave the trolls to get on with the interesting stuff. I wonder which side I imagine I'm on. I think it depends on who I'm standing next to. (And this is where the theory falls down.)

Ultimately, while beauty is undeniably a commodity, so is almost anything else (including ugliness accompanied by good jokes) so people should probably stop making each other miserable and just get on with commodifying themselves as much or as little as they see fit. The accounts girl gets the same amount of money as her colleagues and is married to the middle computer man. In terms of profitable self-commodification, she is no better off than the large lady in her department who is married to the little gnome in membership. In terms of happiness, it's impossible to know, but the accounts girl looks profoundly morose, while the large lady appears chirpy and contented. Maybe the accounts girl knows about the effect of sadness on her face and is waiting for the president to give her a promotion or run off with her.

The membership people are a mixture of nice and nasty. The nicest one is a woman who would rather be working for Greenpeace or the Vegan Society. She has a pathological love of animals. She brings hurt pigeons back from Trafalgar Square and forces the RSPCA to come and take them to the animal hospital. She complains of being overworked and has persuaded the Academy to hire an extra person for her department. The new membership person is a woman who clearly used to ☎ like bullying horses as a child. She treats all people like naughty ponies who have to be kicked in the ribs, jerked at the mouth and whipped. She and the nice woman definitely don't get on. They go to lunch together and pretend to like each other, and then, in the afternoons, the nice lady comes downstairs, near to tears, and tells me that she can't stand it anymore.

In the same room as these these two is a very soft blonde girl, who I can't imagine speaking to, and the little man who is married to the large lady in accounts.

Above this lot (not because they are paid more but simply because they are posher) are the marketing people. They are nice. Well, the two women are nice and the man is a dog. One of the women is about to get married. I'm a bit fascinated by people who want to get married and asked her why. She said she'd been with her fiancé for eleven years so they decided it was about time. Weddings like this must be so boring for the bride and groom. They must wonder what on earth they're doing in front of each other and all their friends and family, wearing stupid clothes, doing something that will change nothing for the better and make it much harder for them to get away from one another. She is far from stupid, though, so I suppose she has her reasons.

The other marketing woman is Indian and recently got married to someone her parents chose for her. Now she has to live in a house with her husband's family. I think she loves him, but not them.

I don't know who I'd rather be. I think I'd rather be myself (a bolshy old cow who will probably never get married to anyone).

*   *   *

Up to the education department, who are perhaps less posh, but who do more serious academic work for the Academy. This is the first department that contains actual Doctors. There are two and a half. One very serious man, one very serious woman and one very unserious, ☎ but smart, boy.

At this point in the hierarchy the characters start losing their definition for me. I almost can't look at the Doctors because I think that they think I'm a bit dense. Because I think this – and have no way of checking my thoughts against reality without coming right out and asking (which I would find impossible) – I'm ashamed of myself in front of them. They are gentle with me and ask how I am, but I feel that if I actually told them (especially about the love thing) they'd be very shocked and embarrassed. I tell them that I'm okay, probably affirming their idea that I'm an imbecile, as anyone who's okay sitting at a desk chirruping ☎☎ the same five words – 'Good morning/afternoon, Academy of Material Science' – three hundred times a day must be at least a little bit thick. ☎☎☎☎

So I don't know the Doctors, and definitely don't understand them, due to some ineffable force in the office set-up that prevents us from really speaking to one another. I think I would like to talk to them more. But because they act as though this sort of contact is out of the question (they definitely seem to believe that I am truly a receptionist) I never find an appropriate moment.

I feel like I'm not supposed to sit with the Doctors in the canteen, although I don't know where I got this idea from. If I see any of the pushers eating and there's a free chair, I always eat with them. But if I see the Doctors eating, no matter how many free chairs there may be, I eat on my own. This is what everyone else does too. The Doctors don't come and sit with the pushers either. People at different levels of the Academy simply don't have lunch together. It makes me mad to watch myself obey this ridiculous convention. I think I do it because I'm afraid

50

the Doctors will be disturbed by me and not like me and will spend the whole meal thinking up strategies to prevent this outrage recurring. But maybe they would be delighted. ☎

The half-Doctor is quite alert to this sort of split and makes it his business to get on with all the pushers. He goes to the pub with them after work and laughs about the Doctors. The pushers like to think the Doctors are a bit inadequate in the field of 'real life'. The half-Doctor allows them to enjoy this joke, knowing perfectly well that if a vital part of 'real life' might be finding out what you like and getting paid for it, the Doctors are doing it much better than the pushers. Some of the Doctors would undoubtedly do their jobs for nothing, due to the fact that they love them so much. They regularly stay in the office well beyond normal working hours without complaining. But, despite the fact that most of them would happily volunteer, they are probably getting paid at least three times as much as their whingeing minions.

The next department, containining yet more Doctors, is publishing. They are some of the most fascinating people in the office to me – perhaps merely because they work on the top floor (which I'm sure I will never see). The only parts of the office I know are the reception and the loo. While the Doctors' jobs sometimes take them to Europe, America and Japan, my job takes me to the bathroom ☎ and back (when I can persuade the printers to let me go).

As I have already mentioned, I have a list of names and extension numbers in front of me. I have some kind of telephone relationship with most of the names on this list. But, because I am quite new to the job, I am still connecting these names and voices with the bodies and faces that pass me during the day. One of the Doctors in the publishing department has a very beautiful bell-like voice. I have had a couple of brief exchanges on the phone with her and, from these, have built up a picture of a perfect doll of a woman. The other day she came down

51

to collect a package and I was forced to realize that she was a little old lady with a bun. The imaginary woman remains so strongly in my mind that I can still never be sure to which one I'm speaking when I hear the tinkling voice on ✂ ☎✍✂ the phone. I have never seen the imaginary woman walk past me. Perhaps a part of me would like to believe that she comes to work by helicopter.

The other publishing person who has really made an impression on me is a rather tall and exceptionally nervous man with a head shaped like a baked bean (with some hopeless wisps of grey hair floating on it). This morning he was anxiously waiting for a parcel to arrive. When parcels arrive I simply look at the name on the label and call the number on the list that corresponds with the name. This isn't generally a problem for me, as I can read. This man, however, got it into his horribly shaped head that this small task might be tricky for someone with a tiny enough brain to qualify as a receptionist. Every time the parcel didn't arrive ☎ (i.e., a lot) he came down to see if I had somehow failed to make the connection between him and it. He would constantly explain in the most stumbling and circuitous manner that he was waiting for a very urgent delivery and that when it came, the way in which I would be able to discover that it was for him would be to check whether or not it had his name on it. He repeatedly told me that his name was Philip Scroll not realizing that, even if I forgot that this particular collection of syllables was supposed to connect with his body, it wouldn't alter anything. All I have to do is match the name on the parcel with the name on the telephone list. Maybe he doesn't want to acknowledge the fact that the letters and numbers ascribed to him are far more important than his face, his body or his brain in terms of our working relationship.

By the time the package arrived I had become quite anxious on his behalf. I called him and told him that a miracle had happened. He and his parcel were now free to unite. He came down and gave me a funny look. Perhaps he'll never talk to me again. Already when he walks past me on his way in and out of the office he turns his back on me (which forces him to walk sideways) and sticks his chin into his collar as if it will make me notice him less. I notice him one of the most of all the people in the office. I wonder what he'd think if he knew. I think I'd like to know him better, but he gets really nervous if I just say hello. By some strange coincidence, almost every time I go to make coffee I find him in the tiny room where the kettle lives. I generally go and hide in the loo until I believe he has finished making his tea as I would find it hard to hang around in a confined space with such a shy and jumpy person. But maybe I could make it my mission to become his friend.

Very near the top of the office is the man who's in charge of all the money. The finance man is in a funny spot. Being the one who deals with the cash, he's a very powerful person in the office hierarchy. But, because he's a mere financier and not an academic, I find myself worrying that the other important figures in the Academy treat him like he's a bit dumb. It amazes me that I should care about this at all but, mysteriously, I do. Despite his being one of the top dogs, I fear that he won't be able to keep up with the lunchtime conversations of his colleagues. I think he suffers. He doesn't really know how to deal with the pushers and flirts very clumsily with the pusher girls. He tries to get matey with the pusher boys, but they don't seem to find him too appealing either. He winks at me in a very gauche way and asks how I am without waiting for an answer. I think he could be quite a nice man but he's definitely in the wrong place. If he was the top money manager in a firm that cared more about money and less about scientific things then people might appreciate him and make way ☎ for the more delicate aspects of his personality. Here he just seems like a rather crass figure who only really understands how to count and act like a cheap version of a man. His secretary, who knows him better than anyone else, insists that he is thoughtful and caring.

How is it that a person whom I find unappealing on every level (physical, conversational and choice of beard shape) can incite so much of my concern? Maybe it's because I identify with him as a misfit at the Academy. He and I and the pigeon lady definitely shouldn't be here. The difference between them and me is that it's perfectly obvious where they ought to be instead. I have absolutely no constructive ideas about where I should go. But perhaps if I gave them the solutions to their situational wrongness they'd be able to return the favour. Somehow, though, I doubt that the financial director of the Academy of Material Science holds the key to my future happiness. But perhaps it's the possibility that he might which makes me so mindful of his well-being.

Now we are really getting to the apex of Institutional importance, to the woman who not only makes vital decisions about bureaucratic stuff, but is also a big-time academic thinker. I believe she is the brain that holds the Academy together. If someone has a problem with one of the other people at work they go and talk to her and she sorts it all out. She clearly has a good understanding of how people function in organizations, and how they can be made to do it better. I'm sure she also knows all about artificial wood.

She has a very unlikely persona for someone of her professional ✂ ✂ ✍ stature. She is an unbearably hesitant speaker. I am often unsure as to whether she is about to speak or whether ☎ she has just fallen asleep with ☎ her eyes ☎ open. I don't dare interrupt her silences in case she is trying to think her way through something important, but I often suspect she may be trying to think her way through something more like a pillow, the fatness and puffiness of which holds her up. I suppose she might be shy (whatever that means). She is the Doctor who I feel I understand the least, although I suspect her mystery may be a ruse put there either by her or by me, and that she is neither more simple nor more complex than anyone else in the office. ✍

*   *   *

The last and absolutely top person in the office, way above the spluttering professor, is the ex-receptionist. Nobody at any level in the entire Academy holds any authority over him. He does whatever he likes. He stopped being the receptionist to help the would-be-fireman assist the office manager, believing this job-change was a promotion. As I have described, the office manager has one of the most odious personalities in London, and the ex-receptionist soon discovered that he was expected to suffer it without a pay-rise. Understandably, he has decided to leave.

Meanwhile he has to work out his month's notice. He is loose in the Academy, not caring at all about what anyone here thinks of him. Nobody can touch him. He tells the chairman that, under no circumstances, will he ever refer to him as Mr Calkin, and continues to call him Baz. He loudly asks the financial director's secretary if he can check her handbag to see how much stuff she shoplifted during her lunch hour. He shows his nipple-rings to visitors. He does endless impersonations of Joaquín Cortes, tapping and twirling up and down the corridor, and wailing at the top of his voice. He tells the office manager to stop ✂☎✂ ✂ ☎ talking out of her arse. He sometimes helps me with the switchboard and I hear him announcing to people that ☎ they'll have to call back in five minutes as the person they need to speak to is having a crap.

He's quite outstanding and should, by rights, be a star, but he has problems with ambition. He says he can't see the point in it any more since so many of his friends have died of AIDS. He claims he can only allow himself to consider his immediate present. He reminds me that the only thing anyone can be sure of in the future is that they are going to ☎ become a corpse. He doesn't seem to feel that what takes place in between his immediate present and his inevitable death makes a large amount of difference.

I see what he means, but I'm not sure I go along with it. In gigantic, universal terms it's clearly correct to say that there isn't that much difference between being notorious in one tiny office, or being notorious in one tiny country, or on one tiny planet. None of these things will prevent you from dying. But the option you choose will radically alter ☎☎☎ the nature of the events that constitute your life. The first option will probably make you moderately poor, the others could make you rich. The first will mean that people who you don't know will generally not know you either, while the second and third will mean that thousands of people who you don't know will have opinions about you. The first will mean that a handful of people will remember you when you're dead, while the two latter could mean that your face and name will be bandied about for the rest of human history. All might ☎ make you happy or unhappy, but it still seems to me like a set of differences worth taking seriously. I realize I am very caught up with evil capitalist notions of merit and social grading as, for no good reason, I believe it's preferable to be a wealthy TV personality than an underpaid office clown. The ex-receptionist is too much for the Academy of Material Science and it makes me mad that he doesn't use his too muchness more profitably. When he finishes here he is going to be a receptionist in an office just around the corner. He will almost certainly be the most exciting person there too. This will probably continue to be how things go with him until he drops dead.

The one salvation I see for him is that other people seem to like to write about him. He doesn't ✂ ☎ even have to do anything terrible. He works as a hairdresser on Saturdays and talks to all the customers. He tells them about his love-life, his pet parrot (to whom he is allergic), his father's miraculous cure at Lourdes, his theories about life and death, etc. And, because this hairdressers' shop is in a part of town densely populated by journalists (Fulham), his stories appear from time to time in newspaper columns. He is always represented as an unlikely character – the journalists are clearly surprised that someone so funny and smart has chosen to cut hair for a living. Like me, they have difficulties understanding people who don't fit comfortably into the hierarchical systems by which most of us are so ✕ ✕ ✕ ✕ ✕ entirely subsumed.

The ex-receptionist is an anti-star, a rare and impressive phenomenon, and I will be interested to see, if he dies in my lifetime, whether the newspapers are inundated with obituaries for him.

↩

I'm afraid this whole office thing sounds far too nineteenth century (not that it shouldn't, I suppose, but I would like to pass for 'a very contemporary writer'). In our office we have a ☎ real live Bartleby (Heck), several of Kafka's naughty office boys (in the postroom), some tragic bachelors (in every single department), and a handful of wretched clerks plucked straight from Gogol (one of them actually lost the tip of his nose in a traffic accident). Who says technology is changing the nature of social relationships?

6

I Find Myself
Feeling Ambivalent

I'm feeling faint-hearted and sentimental again. Last night with the ᨣᨣ was quite lovely. Or at least bits of it were lovely and they made up for the bits that were just ordinary. (I think.) It feels like . . . I don't know what it feels like. After getting in such a state in that café it was quite interesting to watch myself forgiving him instantly and trying to act happy. We both got very drunk in Brixton and went for a walk alongside the railway arches. We found a squashed piece of wire in the shape of a mansion (if you used your imagination). He was nice, but quite untouchable and inexplicably euphoric. It was okay when we were alone but I become quite embarrassed when someone I'm with gets too excitable in public. He was talking nonsense to people in the tube station and they were looking at him like he was completely insane. I think that was the bit I found most off-putting because the rest was mostly fine. I went to see his new home, which is a warehouse with about eleven other people in it (why has he done this to himself again?). His room is okay, but apart from that it's not so good. His housemates insist on holding meetings to discuss the most boring things and the toilet and shower are outdoors. Still, I almost enjoyed staying there (in an anthropological way).

At work today, I'm in trouble. I'm feeling pretty anxious. I can only stay a good girl for a very definite period and then all my nonsense starts to show. (It's my 'inability to stick to rules' – even when I really want to. Bloody jet-setting parents.)

Yesterday was a calamity and today it's got worse. I don't seem to know how to conduct myself in an office environment. From the outside I imagined that offices were places where everyone had to act like impeccable automatons until they either got M.E., R.S.I., cancer or heart disease, at which point they were forced to take time off for a re-think. This doesn't seem to be strictly true. (I was being a bit harsh and puritanical.) It's perfectly clear with almost all of the people here that whatever they are is surplus to their job requirements. They are to their jobs what a very fat lady would be to a tissue-paper corset. They're exploding all over the office.

I'm starting to like nearly all of them – especially the marketing people and the nice pigeon lady in membership who really loves talking about romantic stuff and is an excellent confidante. I'm even getting on better with Philip Scroll since I have been forcing myself to talk to him in the tea room. The real ice-breaker came yesterday when we were washing our cups while the kettle boiled. We both decided against using the grimy, bacteria farm of a sponge in favour of scrubbing with our fingers. In condemning the sponge we both said at almost exactly the same time that it wasn't an object we would want to contemplate. I guess when you say the same thing at the same time as someone else it makes you believe you might have other things in common. This simultaneous non-contemplation of the sponge has meant that Philip now smiles and says hello instead of scuttling past like a self-conscious crab. He still seems very twitchy and freaked out, but I suppose that's just who he is and I shouldn't take it personally. The next time I see him eating on his own I might even experiment with having lunch with him. But it looks like I might not be here for long. Yesterday I really messed up. I was in a funny mood anyway and I just let things slip. *Now* I can't understand why I encouraged a friend who came in to see me to play games on the computer. I don't know how I allowed the ∧∧∧∧ to jump on my desk. Any other day I would have done it differently, but yesterday

I didn't seem to care. The pair of them hung about looking unbusinesslike and everybody saw. Just before it all happened I'd asked the personnel woman if I could stay here a while (so I could get on with this) and she seemed to think it might be possible. But then I bollocksed it all in front of everyone in the afternoon. Now they know I'm not perfect (although I'm sure they still believe I am a receptionist).

My crimes seem so unbelievably miniscule to me, but to the office manager they are diabolical. For once someone other than her has actually done something wrong, so she can really get sanctimonious and mean it. Today she is wearing a matching skirt and top. Well, the skirt and top match each other, but are made from a fabric that definitely doesn't match itself. It's a synthetic satin textured with shiny dots, with a plaid background in black, white and brown, and big, splashy purple, green and orange orchids floating over the top. The skirt is pleated and the top is too tight across her tits. It's very hard to accept a telling-off from someone wearing this outfit. She says the old geezer saw my appalling behaviour on the surveillance monitors. The version she heard was that I had allowed a cycle messenger to run around on my desk as part of a shameless flirtation ritual. This, apparently, was absolutely unacceptable behaviour. 'The Academy is not a dating agency,' she told me. 'You're here to do a job and if you can't do it sensibly then we can easily get someone else.'

I know I am replaceable, but I can't stand to be reminded. I like to maintain a fantasy that I am special, even in my receptionist role, and that people would be sad if I disappeared. The office manager seems to take an active pleasure in disillusioning me. She likes to let me know that, to her, I am just a body housing a collection of neurones which barely make me capable of connecting calls and handing out visitors' badges. I find her reminders of my replaceability intolerably aggressive and, as a result, find myself slipping into long, involved reveries during which I slowly torture her. This is one of the few occasions at the Academy where I actually get to use my education, so I really go to town. I pummel her with two thousand years' worth of punishment techniques ranging from crucifixion and flaying to Chinese aural tortures and disembowelment by rat, followed by the entire machinery of the Spanish Inquisition, stocks, garottes, racks, thumb screws and iron maidens and finishing with a hard spell of cabinet-making on a diet of mouldy gruel.

What actually happened yesterday, as I have already mentioned in passing, was that the MMM dropped in to tell me he'd got a temporary job as a bike courier and that he wasn't going to leave the country any more. He followed this piece of excellent news by jumping on my desk in order to take an aerial-view photograph of the reception area. I don't really know why he did this, so I can hardly justify it to someone else. He *is* an artist, a fact which could probably be used to explain a lot of things – although not to the office manager (and I shouldn't really be telling you either). I might want to think he was performing a bit of shameless flirtation, but it didn't seem like it at the time. It seemed more like a sure sign of his loopiness and careless lack of respect for me and for the unfortunate position I have landed myself in. I begged him not to jump on the desk, but he carried on regardless, silently suggesting that I was a bit pathetic and unnecessarily restrained. This is easy for him to feel as he doesn't have to be yelled at for half an hour by a woman in a horror-suit. The whole scene was not something I felt like discussing with the office manager, so I just let her carry on believing I was a bimbo whose most engaging pastime was to entice men carrying packages.

The Academy has transformed itself back into the kind of hell-palace I'd envisaged before I came. Like a policeman who manages to appear personable until you're suspected of foul play, the office has turned from ineffectual and sweet to fierce and grim without any warning. I don't know what the office manager has said, but some of the people in the accounts department have started giving me funny looks. I'm too fat for this particular corset. (Why can fat people and old people defend their rights, but not people with erratic temperaments? Of course I mess up – I was designed to. Everyone was. But the trick is clearly to hide it until you can make your way into an authority position and then to start punishing everyone else for your own failings. I know it's cod-psychology – which I love – but I think that's really what happens. In my daydreams I am going to have to punish the office manager doubly for being a walking psychological cliché.)

What will I do if I lose my job? I can't even claim dole as I have twice already been refused housing benefit for my flat. Sometimes I wish I wanted to be a film maker rather than a writer. When Fassbinder ran out of money he would send members of his cast out to prostitute themselves. I wish I had a cast of real people on whom I could rely to get cash to help me finish this. I wish I could use some of the staff at the Academy. The office manager could do correction for naughty boys, the would-be-fireman could pose for some saucy uniform porn shots and the nice computer nerd could freelance as a web designer doing flesh sites on the Internet. Meanwhile I could stay at home and write without interruption. However, the sad fact is that now I might lose my job I have almost started to like it. I would hate to sit at home like a miserable, lonely writer and have to make things up.

⁓

I'd love to tell you more about these last few weeks leading up to my present romantic crisis, but I'm compelled to go on a bit more about what's happening now. I'm feeling all ambivalent, and I'm not quite sure why. There are still big traces of the love thing, but I'm having all these doubts. I can't decide whether this is an appropriate moment to cop out, or whether this is the bit where you make things good by persevering. I think I'll take the second option (if I'm the one who decides – maybe I'm not the only one with this feelingless feeling), partly because I'm still not prepared to let go of my expectations and partly because it does seem a bit monstrous to give up on something simply because of a glimmer of imperfection (although I think it may be more than a glimmer). I'm actually finding this bit hard to say because the more I think about the MMM, the more the love thing (and especially the lust thing) comes back. I felt quite nonplussed by him last night, but after my solitary tantrum in the café when he failed to show up I found it hard to switch immediately over to warm and tender emotions. He *was* really self-absorbed and hard to relate to, but I guess he's not the only nutcase in this relationship – something I must try to bear in mind.

I think I might be trying to make too much sense of a senseless thing. If I try to describe it sort of more like how it feels I'd say that I still feel quite smitten and can't stop thinking about the sex and the sweeter aspects of his character, but I'm rather worried by the more difficult things about him. Why does he sometimes behave so oddly? And why does he want to meet so infrequently when meeting can be so good? I feel like I need to spend more time with him to turn him (for myself, but alas not for you) into a more well-rounded and fleshed-out character. Right now I feel like he's only choosing to show what he wants to show. And I think I might be getting a bit fed up with it. I need to see more personal stuff before I can take him seriously. I wonder why he's being so reluctant. Maybe I could keep him prisoner for a fortnight for the purpose of dragging his personal stuff out.

⌒

Funny how self-critical lunch can make you. I'm not sure I can carry on where I left off. What has made me feel so different?

Does having a lump of food in your stomach modify your ideas and beliefs? Or is it the time-lapse that makes the difference? I'm not who I was before I ate my sandwiches. What I wrote only an hour ago seems like nonsense to me.

It must either happen because my pre-lunch low blood-sugar level makes me ratty and prone to irrational thoughts or because, during my free hour, I have time to work through whatever misguided notions I was stewing in all morning. Actually, I think it's the combination of the two as, if I only do one or the other, I can sometimes stay stuck in my pre-lunch persona all afternoon. I think I may also feel a bit different because of another brief chat I had with Philip in the tea room. He is a truly weird person. He makes the ⌁ seem like a plain, well-adjusted young man. It's not that he says or does anything explicitly strange (like jump on tables). He just gives the very strong impression of someone who is making a huge internal effort to appear halfway normal. It's as if his frigid and timorous exterior is camouflaging an exuberant and possibly very frightening inner existence. After speaking briefly to Philip about the weather my emotional problems seem like playground stuff. Whatever is going on inside him suddenly seems ten times more fascinating that the harmless mental meanderings going on inside me. Philip has put me back in my place.

Now I feel like a TV that has been re-tuned. I'm refreshed and better. But I still have to show the same programmes. So here's a clearer, brighter picture of what's going on.

∽

I can see that the problem with the personal stuff is that most people's is quite hard to deal with and it's no wonder they want to keep it under wraps. But when it's someone you're trying to be in love with it's not the same. If all they let you see of them is what everyone else sees, then it's pretty pointless to pretend that anything special is happening – apart from in

64

your imagination. At the moment the ᴍᴡᴡᴍ remains a mere screen for my projections and I'm really just bored with myself and would like *him* to change the picture.

I wonder what's making me so interested in films and tellys today.

I can't understand why I find it so hard to talk with him. The crying episode that caused me to fall in love really made me feel like he was the kind of person I'd be able to say anything to. Maybe I was just mistaken. Or maybe I actually could say things to him if I could only think of what they are when he's there. The imaginary conversations I have with him are definitely a good deal better than the real ones. I think he makes me feel something so strongly that I can't quite explain it. I probably don't even want to in case he sneers and tells me to stop being ridiculous. I desperately want to know him better, but I can't work out how to do it. Sometimes I wish I was still a child and could just go up to other children, start babbling, knock them round the head a bit, get a kick in the shin and declare ourselves best friends. Being an adult can feel so cripplingly strategic sometimes.

I've got this desperate urge to tell the truth right now but I can't seem to work out what it is. I'm aware that if you only do it half-way you sound like a women's magazine writer. That's what a lot of this is like, isn't it? I wonder why it's so easy to be glib, and so hard not to be. Nobody really wants to be glib, do they? But most of us are most of the time. Anything else is just so difficult. As soon as you start trying not to be, the world becomes a very unsteady environment. Sometimes I feel physically sick when I try seriously to think about what on earth's going on. I feel so strange, but at the same time I'm sure that this strange feeling is very, very normal. Is it a by-product of the love thing? And why would that be true? It's certainly true that when I fall in love I start asking all sorts of probably unnecessary questions. Not even in a way that I'm in control of. It's more as though being in love throws everything into question. And, quite frankly, it scares me to death. It makes me want to keep checking that everything's okay. I have this tendency to want to make everything boring. I love the manic fervour of falling in love, but it sort of tips me over to a point where I can't stand it any more and I have either to get out (by deciding that my chosen object is unworthy of such overpowering emotion), or I have to domesticate (read castrate) them. It's awful. What do I do? What do you do? How does a person ever know what to do? Why are my tiny little problems giving me such enormous amounts of grief? How are you, I wonder?

7

Stopping and Starting

Why are endings so difficult? Is the reason I have stuck with my boyfriend this long that I'm afraid of being alone? Why didn't I act earlier, when I first felt something was wrong? I think it started to go funny about three years ago, but here we are today, still sharing the same bed. It's unbearable to come home to him each night when I am having such strong feelings about somebody else.

I think I might find the idea of terminating the relationship itself quite appealing. It's the other consequences that I find scary. What will happen to our home and our mutual friends? I wonder whether I'm using these as an excuse. Maybe I need him more than I like to recognize. Perhaps I use the house and the friends as symbols for a deeper attachment. What do I actually feel about him? I don't seem to know.

My boyfriend is an endearing version of the well-mannered English gentleman. He is also very funny and brilliant – facts which I must stress as I would hate to caricature a person I have spent so much time with. He has shortish, dark hair, wears a fair amount of corduroy, and writes super-serious (and as yet unpublished) spy thrillers. He also works in a library. I know this might make him sound a bit boring but, really, he isn't. I mean, I can get a bit bored with him now that we've been together, getting on each other's nerves, for so long. But people who meet him for the first time usually think he's nice. He has an unlikely high-pitched laugh and is generally very personable and good natured. I think the sad truth is that he's much better in superficial situations than he is at close quarters. When you've been around him for a while you realize that he doesn't change much – that all he knows how to do is deal with people like he's at a permanent tea party. He can talk seriously and make jokes and everything, but he can't yell or get too passionate. The advantage is that he's never embarrassing, but the disadvantage is that he isn't exactly exciting either. I feel a lot for him, but I'm coming to the conclusion that the things I feel aren't the kind of feelings that really get me going. Our sex life is terrible. Both of us would rather read a book. We can skip sex for months and I don't even notice. It makes me feel like an old lady. The fact is that the idea of having sex with him makes me feel ill. I just can't see him as a sexy person any more (or myself when I'm with him for that matter). It would be like having sex with a weetabix, just completely wrong. I think it's because he's always claiming to be ill with something or another and I've got used to the idea of his body being a problem rather than anything desirable or good. He also makes love very discreetly, without looking at me or speaking. I hate it. We're really good friends until we have sex and then it's as if he suddenly starts ignoring me. I find it so disturbing that I can hardly talk to him about it so I just end up avoiding the issue altogether. I suppose that's why I've gone so mad about the ∧∧∧ – I needed to find an obstreperous bloke I could get a bit delirious over to save me from a life of emotional destitution.

I told my boyfriend about the ∧∧∧ straight after the crying thing. He just said oh dear and looked annoyed. I think I still thought that there might be a chance of saving the relationship. I didn't feel it was possible to drop everything immediately just because of one small (but dramatic) incident. Maybe a part of me wanted a dramatic response from my boyfriend. But dramatic responses are absolutely excluded from his stock of skills. He has other ways of going about things, most of which are not perceptible to outsiders – including me. As far as I know, the only times he ever speaks his mind are when I have my ears under the bathwater or when I am drying my hair. If I ask him to repeat what he has just said he looks at me incredulously and says 'no way'.

The whole week after the crying incident, we carried on acting like nothing was different. We even bought a rug together. We never addressed the fact that what was happening might be capable of seriously affecting us. It was as if we didn't want to know. It seemed too incredible to think that the 〰〰, about whom I previously had no strong feelings, could perform an action that carried a meaning that could persuade me to dismantle both mine and my boyfriend's present existences. Especially as I wasn't sure I'd ever see him again.

Luckily, as you know, I bumped into him a week later. After staying at the 〰〰 's house, I came back and told the boyfriend straight away. He told me I was a stinker and went back to sleep. Since then we have been failing to think up ways of dealing with both the emotional and material problems of separation. One idea he came up with was that we could carry on living together, but turn one of our other rooms into a bedroom so we could lead more separate lives. Something tells me this plan is unrealistic. The only thing in its favour is that this new room wouldn't necessarily have to be painted white.

I fell for my boyfriend five years ago and waited a year before doing anything about it. One similarity between the beginning of the 〰〰 story and this one was that I knew of his existence for quite a while before falling for him: I didn't find him attractive until I saw something he'd written, after which I became obsessed. It wasn't a whole spy saga, just a short thing that seemed desperately romantic in a repressed kind of way. I think I believed I would be able to unbridle the frenzied passion lurking underneath. Falling in love can be like that, can't it? You're more interested in the poten-tial person than the one you actually meet. If I'd wanted a Heathcliffy boyfriend, why not just hold out for one, rather than getting an Edgar Linton and hoping to do some work on him?

At the beginning of the relationship it really seemed to me like a big deal. I felt he was someone I wanted to stay with for a long time. I think there is a problem with deciding this at the start. How can you possibly know? After about three months I began asking whether he thought we'd be together in ten years. He would say he had no idea. I would say that I couldn't possibly imagine it, but I found the idea of splitting up unbearably painful. However, if we weren't going to be together in ten years, we were going to have to fall out at some point. I would get very upset and suggest (without meaning it) that we go our separate ways at once. It was as if I wanted to ruin our present by dragging in all these worries about our future. I'm not entirely sure what interest I had in doing this. I think, partly, I felt that a long relationship was a kind of closure. I was more caught up with fantasies of what was being prevented from happening than with what was actually happening. I was hardly *there* at all. Perhaps I was afraid of having something to lose, so I didn't allow myself ever actually to have it. This was not a tactic that made either of us happy. It was a definite case of causing pain by trying to avoid it.

〜

It seems we are brought up with certain difficulties we have to overcome if we are to have any hope of ever being happy. The problem of how to form attachments is one of my biggest concerns. I know that at the beginning I presented it like I wasn't at all responsible and that it was a fundamental flaw in the design of my character, but obviously it isn't so simple. I have, loitering somewhere at the back of my brain, a new, improved, restored and updated model of myself which I am endlessly aspiring towards – a straightforwardly warm and honest specimen rather than the dodgy ball of angst I am at the moment. I would have liked it if my boyfriend had been able to help me out with a few renovations. Instead he would simply tell me to stop worrying, and that would be the end of the conversation. I hated it. I think you might as well drop dead on the spot if you can't be bothered to change. I know these days it's normal to believe that all problems have to be dealt with on your own terms, but I am old-fashioned enough to believe that other people may be able to affect me. I think this boyfriend was not the person to help me get over my difficulties (and equally that I wasn't the person to help him out with his). He has a very small vocabulary for speaking about feelings, making it hard to discuss whatever's going on. When something starts going a bit funny, it's very difficult to do anything about it. He makes me feel like a nutcase for expecting more from our relationship than we're getting. If I ever suggest that things might not be perfect he hints that I might only be thinking this because I am mad.

Conversely, I believe all this is what has kept us together so long. The whole thing is built on a silent contract to reduce suffering, making it apparently very safe and easy. (Although, at the same time, this contract ensures that my boyfriend has a permanent ache and that I always feel profoundly wrong.) We have only ever had two real rows, and one of them was about eating sweets too quickly.

I once asked my mum for a bit of guidance and she was useless. It's amazing how experts can't deal with their own families. She just said that we probably needed a holiday.

My boyfriend seems to find it funny that I am writing a book. Perhaps this bit of superciliousness will be the thing that makes me capable of hating him enough to give up my lovely home.

ᔆ

I wonder what will happen if the ∧∧∧ and I really do fall in love. Will I go through all the same crappy stuff again? What does it mean to change your boyfriend? Is it healthy to switch partners every once in a while just for the sake of keeping life interesting, or is it more exciting to stick with the same person and work things out? Am I running away from my problems (and hence straight back into them) or am I making a brave decision to move on? How can I know whether I'm doing the right thing until I've done it, by which time I'll be stuck with it anyhow?

The MMM is very different to the boyfriend. While the boyfriend is keen to hide and subdue his emotions, the MMM seems to display feeling quite readily (although it isn't always easy to understand what these strange outbursts of feelingful behaviour mean). The boyfriend is polite while the MMM can be quite rude. The boyfriend is pretty while the MMM is handsome. The boyfriend is apparently stable while the MMM seems quite unstable. Are these kinds of difference enough to change the way *I* behave? It's funny to be ending and beginning at the same time. What I can't work out is how much the way I relate to people depends on my history, and how much it depends on them. I hope I am able to do things differently this time, but what will it take to change me? I wish the MMM could stop my twisted unconscious getting up to its usual tricks. What would happen then? I suppose it would either think up some new ones, specially designed for him, or I would be saved and live happily ever after. I'm going to have to sort the talking thing out, though, if this is going to happen. It's ironic that I should be out of love with my boyfriend because he can't seem to deal with the more intimate, peculiar aspects of being a person, and infatuated with the MMM because he's openly odd, while the truth is that I can't *really* talk to either of them. Perhaps this is the sign I need to tell me I am merely running away from something I'd be better off sticking around and trying to deal with.

Why do I believe so strongly in the person I thought the MMM was when I first went home with him? People are always faking in order to get each other into bed. I'm suddenly scared that my belief in the MMM's merit is completely dumb. A friend of a friend used to go out with an actor who had played Gandhi in a film. Apparently people identified him so much with the role that they would treat him like he was this amazing guy who'd done all this great stuff for the people of India, showing him tons of completely undue respect. Maybe this is what I am doing to the MMM.

8

Philip Scroll

I just had lunch with Philip Scroll! It was fantastic in a sort of unfantastic way. I went to the canteen with my book, ready to eat alone if I had to, and there he was by himself. The whole time I was in the queue with my tray I couldn't decide whether to do it or not. He is a Doctor, so it would have been quite acceptable to ignore the empty seat next to him and go and sit alone elsewhere.

I've become so curious about him that I decided I couldn't pass up an opportunity to corner him. When I'd got my food I went up to his table and asked if he'd mind if I joined him. For a split second he looked at me like I'd punched him in the eye. Then he smiled – more at the table than at me – and said no. I sat down and realized pretty quickly that I didn't have much to say. He looked really flustered and started moving things around as if he was trying to give me more space or something. I find it amazing when older people are shy. Shyness seems to me like something you ought to have given up by the age of twenty-six at the latest – or at least transformed into a cool, reserved manner. I told him not to worry about clearing the table on my behalf. He asked me what I was having for lunch, even though it was perfectly obvious that it was a slice of damp quiche. I noticed he was eating a haricot bean salad, which seemed a bit cannibalistic.

When I meet people more nervous than me I try to treat them in the way I would wish to be treated when I am being a jittery prat. Instead of letting them put me on edge I try to

74

show them that I'm not at all worried by their fretfulness. I make it clear to them that their jumpiness doesn't put me off. I think it's because, once I realize they're more scared of me than I am of them, I can relax with them (like with spiders). I quite enjoy talking to really shaky types because they make me feel like exactly the opposite kind of person to the one I normally imagine I am. When I talk to the MMM or to most of the Doctors at the Academy I feel like a loose flake of dandruff. But when I talk to a fragile construction like Philip I feel like a chunk of Stonehenge. I decided the best way to calm him down would be to ask him about his job. He answered that at the moment he was editing about half of the Academy's publications, including the journal in which I had read the article about plastic wood. I told him I thought it was quite an interesting article, although I didn't know whether it was because it was about an interesting substance, or because someone had actually written a whole article about something so obviously boring. Whichever way, by the end of the article I was pretty interested. He turned away and tittered into his shoulder furthest from me. It was a guilty laugh, as if I had blasphemed the God of polymers. In order to redeem himself he tried to get serious and said that Material Science was a fascinating subject. He got a real ramble on about plastic cups and I wasn't sure whether or not to stop him. I couldn't decide whether it was going to be better to encourage him to speak about the things he was naturally drawn to or to try to change the subject. How do you make friends with a person who is willing to talk at length about the production methods of disposable beakers? At first I tried to interject with questions, just to show that I was listening. But then I realized this wasn't necessary. The whole time he talked I watched him super-concentratedly, as if looking at him could tell me something about him he wasn't telling me outright. He was saying something about a visit he had made to a factory. It was true that I wasn't altogether mesmerized by the actual conversation, but with Philip it isn't what he says that makes him interesting, but what you imagine he's feeling or saying to himself as he speaks to you. He always looks as though he knows he is being a bit tedious but fears that if he talked about the things he was actually interested in you would want to know him even less. I'm quite sure he is wrong about this but don't know what to do about it. His body looks very weak, although not strictly unhealthy. He is quite thin and his skin – particularly on his hands and neck – seems a bit too loose for him. He also dresses rather fascinatingly, but you have to get quite close up to notice. As he was rabbiting on I saw that absolutely everything he wore was synthetic. I wonder whether he has an aversion to all things not resulting from modern science.

When he finally finished with the cups he asked me what it was like to be a receptionist. I told him it wasn't exactly riveting, but that I wasn't planning on doing it for long. He said it was a shame as I seemed to be a very good one. If it had been anyone else I would have got up and left at once, but from someone as gauche as Philip this sort of backhandedness arrives without a trace of ill will. He is clearly too busy trying to act like an ordinary human being to have time to think about directing surreptitious insults at others.

He asked me what I had been doing before and I told him about my MA. At first I said it was in history, but when he asked me which period I decided to tell him the truth. Usually when I tell people they either say 'oh' and think nothing of it or are repulsed and tell me I must be sick. When I told Philip he looked very impressed and interested. I told him about my thesis – *The Spectacle of Death: the changing ethics of public execution – the State, the Church and the crowd*. He said it sounded fascinating, but the subject that really interested him was the sixteenth century, with its elaborate torture machines.

Just as I realized he and I might really have something to talk about we were joined by the already-married marketing lady. I would have felt a bit funny carrying on with the punishment thing in front of somebody else, so I was relieved when he dropped it too. She said something friendly and innocuous about what a horrible day it was outside. We all agreed and then fell silent for a few seconds. Philip is clearly one of those people who choose to take the blame for silences. He stood up suddenly, knocking his chair over backwards and mumbled something about leaving us to get on. He rushed out before I had a chance to say goodbye. I hope he doesn't get embarrassed about the stupid way in which he left and stop speaking to me.

I asked the marketing lady what she thought of him and she was pretty diplomatic about his oddness. She just said she didn't know him but that he seemed all-right. She said he had been at the Academy for twenty-five years. I asked her if she didn't find that a bit extraordinary and she said yes. I also asked her if he was married and she laughed and said, 'What do you think?' I said that I thought he probably was, just to make her laugh even more. I wonder why it's so obvious that he's a bachelor and why the way in which it's obvious is a laughing matter for others. I like the marketing lady, but I didn't like the way she laughed so much about Philip's singleness – even though I'd caused her to do it. I told her about my run-in with the office manager in order to redirect the bitching towards a more deserving subject. When I got back to my desk the would-be-fireman somehow knew that I had had lunch with Philip – whom he calls Norman Bates. He asked me how my date went and said it wasn't a good idea to go all the way on the first afternoon. He also told me to watch out in the shower. Luckily he had his hand resting on the arm of my swivel chair so I could crash down on it really hard with the spine of my hardbacked book. When he finally stopped whinging and pretending to be mortally wounded he strolled off down the corridor making the repeated squeaking sound from *Psycho*.

9

Libel

My father has the keys to my flat and comes to stay from time to time when he has something to do in London. He is always arranging meetings with shampoo companies, or obscure chemical manufacturers, or going down to the Patent Office to make sure that, whatever it is, he does it first. This is a very non-ideal arrangement, but I like my dad so I don't want to make a fuss about it.

On my table yesterday was a print-out of all the stuff I have written so far. When I got home my father was there. He told me he had read my manuscript. I was mildly annoyed and embarrassed, but I sort of figured that, as it was a novel, I could hardly say it was private. (I really only meant it for strangers, though.) He said he found it quite entertaining but that, if it ever got published, it would get me into trouble. He told me it was a bit naïve to think I could say whatever I liked about anyone. He said the bits about the Academy were libellous and that I should watch out.

This had never crossed my mind, and I found it worrying. What if I actually wrote something good and then couldn't publish it because all the characters would sue? Why did my father have to tell me this? Why didn't he just give me some fatherly advice about my romantic problems? I know he's trying to keep me out of trouble, but this is typical of the way he goes about things. Instead of talking about the stuff that's really getting to me, he turns the whole thing into a legal issue. Sometimes I get really shocked when I remember that my dad is just a classic, inhuman science guy. You might think that scientists' wives and children can cut through all their crap, but you're wrong. My dad might burp and stink up the bathroom, but that's about as human as he gets. Everything in life is just a technical problem for him.

Now I feel completely stuck. Either I have to change all the characters a bit so that they won't be recognizable as themselves, or I have to ignore his warning and deal with the outcome. What shall I do? The people at the Academy seem particularly amazing to me and I feel that if I change them for a cast of made-up people they won't be as good. In real life I may want to swap them for a selection of my own choice (I would invite Elizabeth Taylor to be the office manager), but here I think they're better left the same. One WWW is bad enough, I can't let the rest of the cast walk out on me.

The dumb thing about libel is that, if you describe someone accurately and truthfully they can't take you to court, however horrible you make them sound. But if you warp and twist and unfairly insult them, they can. The bit I don't get is that, if they feel that the person you have described is not like them, why would they want to identify themselves with it in order to say that they are different? I suppose it's tricky in this case because the people are being identified by their position in the company as well as by their behaviour. Maybe I could switch all their jobs around and change the name of the Academy and its departments. But I'm very concerned with descibing exactly what's going on around me and am not much interested in messing about with it. I remember when I went to art classes I was told to look carefully at whatever I was drawing and to try not to draw it like I expected it to be. They said this was the only way to make the drawing end up looking like the thing. If I didn't do this, but just used my prior knowledge of the object, I would apparently get a wonky, bad drawing that looked like something trying pitiably to look like the thing. If

I start playing around with the Academy, changing everyone into the kind of person I imagine works in an office, I'm afraid I might end up with something clumsy and unrealistic. Should I care about this more than I care about the reputations and feelings of the people I'm describing?

I think the Academy should be grateful for the service I am providing. In the hall they have photographs of all their past presidents, but no pictures of any of the other staff. They are clearly concerned with posterity, but don't give a shit about remembering anyone else in the company. Why not have portraits of all their old receptionists? At least now there will exist, for better or worse, a record of some of the other people who worked here. I apologize to the office manager for being so mean, but at least she can be glad that she has been immortalized.

～

I just spoke to a friend who told me that all novels are built out of a collection of the author's family, friends and acquaintances and that hardly anyone ever bothers to sue. This strikes me as very true. Maybe my father is worried about something else. Maybe he is worried that I will destroy my own reputation by giving away all my secrets. Perhaps he doesn't like it that I have a sexy boyfriend rather than the dad-friendly pancake I had before. Maybe he is worried that I will destroy *his* reputation by exposing him as a bad parent. Maybe he really does feel sorry about me being so nervy and fucked up. He shouldn't feel *too* bad because I have every hope of improving.

His warning is causing me to suffer all sorts of terrible guilt and anxiety so I have decided to ignore it and ban him from reading my manuscript ever again.

And, anyhow, what's the point in someone reading it prematurely if they don't even have anything useful to say about the love stuff?

10

Visitors

While I may be growing to love some of the people at the Academy, I am less sure of how I feel about the visitors. The visitors come in three main types: old men who are here for a conference, friends or partners of employees, and sales people. There is also the occasional Lord or Sir who the secretaries all enjoy getting in a flap about. The Queen's husband is apparently coming to the Academy in a couple of weeks too.

The old men, who make up the overwhelming bulk of all visitors, look roughly the same as one another, but behave quite differently. Some are chatty and personable, some are brisk and efficient, some are scatty and comical, and some are rude and obnoxious.

Sometimes one of the old men asks if one of the other old men has arrived yet. I tell him to look in the visitors' book to see if he can find the name. Some of the old men have rather dodgy handwriting and it isn't always possible to tell from the visitors' book who's here and who isn't. If the first old man can't spot the second old man's name, he begins to give a physical description of him. The description tends to go something like this; shortish grey hair, about average height, Burberry mac, moustache, sometimes wears a tweed hat. It is impossible for me to tell from this description whether their particular old man is here yet. I ask for more details (an oddity perhaps) and they look at me, dumbfounded, and confess that they can't come up with one. I ask what their colleague is like, to see if I can recognize him from a description of his temperament.

81

Sometimes they say things like, 'He has a great sense of humour and a kind of wicked laugh.' I wonder who on earth they can possibly mean, but say it's possible that there is a visitor who fits this description. Later I see them leaving for lunch with some crotchety old bugger and am forced to face the fact that we are all different in different circumstances. While this second old man may choose to be horrible to me, he chooses to be humorous and wicked with his friend.

I often feel that people are at their most ridiculous when dealing with receptionists. They tend either to display a too nice or too nasty version of their normal persona. Maybe they find the encounter embarrassing. I think this might be because the receptionist is the person they *have* to see before the person they *want* to see. The too nice ones attempt to compensate for the sad fact that I could be anyone (while the person they have come to see is specific). They try desperately to make the encounter 'human' by telling me all sorts of uninteresting details about their train journey or by complimenting me on my hairstyle. The too nasty ones deal with the same problem in the opposite way. They seem to want to make me suffer the fact that I am entirely unimportant to them. They overact nastiness, perhaps because they don't know how else to deal with the situation. They seem to be traumatized by the fact that I am a human being and not a robot. Perhaps both types are upset by the sight of a fellow-member of their species doing something that requires skill-levels so far below average human capacity. They recognize, unconsciously, that there must be an enormous gap between what I am doing and who I actually am. They don't know what to do about this unaccounted-for bit, so they try either to address it (and find that it isn't necessarily that easy) or they try to obliterate all knowledge of it.

I tend to mimic their treatment of me, perhaps because I don't know what to do about their unaccounted parts either. If they are nice, I try to be nice, and if they are nasty, I'm nasty back.

I wonder if they ever describe me to one another.

People who aren't here on business tend to have a different attitude towards me. Partners and friends of employees are generally more relaxed and personable than the old men.

I am usually quite surprised when I meet people's partners. I never notice myself thinking about who they could be in advance, but I find that when they appear they are never who I would have pictured if I had tried to guess what they would be like. I was amazed to discover that one of the most prim and upright secretaries had a husband like Grizzly Adams. And that a rather mouse-like man in accounts is married to a vivacious, blonde keep-fit instructor.

It becomes clearer to me when I meet their partners that, at home, the people at the Academy become something other than whatever they are throughout the day. It's a relief to me to think of the stiff, nervy secretary in the arms of a rugged, kind-looking man. It makes me feel less disturbed by the whole office set up. Perhaps, after all, these people *do* find a place to work out some of their excess stuff. Maybe it *is* possible to have a job and continue to have a life.

I like to meet people's partners and friends and always chat to them and give them special treatment.

The third category of visitors is sales people. These are a very mixed bunch. Sometimes they just want to drop off some promotional information and then leave. When this happens, I just chuck whatever they give me straight into the dustbin. I used to try to pass it on because I felt sorry for them. But this just meant that someone else had to dispose of it, so I decided it was best to cut out the middle-man and do it myself. I'm sure this is what all receptionists do. Who is supposed to benefit from this preposterous scheme?

There is another, more successful, breed of sales person. These ones target select members of staff and bribe them with gifts. If the person in charge of buying the Academy's envelopes is told that they, personally, will receive a free bottle of champagne for every ten thousand envelopes the Academy uses, they generally accept the offer. They build up a relationship with their benefactor who, in turn, persuades them to buy as much stuff as possible. To do this type of sales job well you need to be both forceful and charming. It is interesting to watch how sales people attempt to combine these two characteristics.

One of the most regular sales visitors is a woman who sells postage stuff. She does the charming side of her job with her outfits – striking combinations of leopard prints, transparent fabrics, leather and lashings of make-up – and does the forceful side with her speech: she tells people what to do while they are hypnotized by her clothes. It certainly works on the would-be-fireman. He is always receiving small, mysterious gifts from her in return for large sums of the Academy's money.

There is another sales person who I find quite frightening. He seems to have no charm whatsoever. I have no idea what he sells. When he comes, he gives me a menacing look and asks to speak to a person who no longer works here. He has done this twice in the short time I have been here. When I tell him that the person has left, he looks very angry. He tells me he needs to speak to someone at once. Last time he came I called one of the marketing women. She came to collect him and took him to her office. After he left she raced up to tell me to let her know immediately if he ever reappeared. I asked her who he was but she refused to tell me. Mysteries like this drive me crazy. I'm desperate to know what he's up to. I'd like to believe he is running a huge protection racket. I hope he comes back soon.

11

Evil

How come this love business makes me so mad? I know it's not unusual: it's perfectly commonplace for people to kill themselves and each other over comparatively minor romantic disappointments – provided their biographical co-ordinates are set in the right positions. I don't really know where mine are set because I've always laboured under the impression that I'm the most ordinary, polite, well-meaning type of girl. But now I realize there are chinks in that story. I'm only just starting to believe that I might be capable of quite horrible things. And I really don't know what to do about it.

It's not even simply in romantic situations that I am a potential menace. Look at how I feel about the office manager. Maybe I am a monster and just don't know it yet. All psychopaths presumably have a period before they actually perform their evil deeds. My first real insight into how horrible I might be came when I was nineteen. When I was seventeen I disappeared from home for quite a while. When I was eighteen I came back. And when I turned nineteen my parents left home and I stayed behind. At first it seemed like quite a good thing – I had this great big flat all to myself and it could have been brilliant but I started going a bit nuts. Daytimes were fine but night-time was repulsive. I'd start getting jittery as soon as the sun went down and either have to watch the telly, keeping my hand on the remote control buttons in case of anything even slightly disturbing (a strange camera angle, a dimly lit room, atmospheric music) or I'd try to put myself to bed – which would invariably be an absolute disaster. I just couldn't stop thinking horrible thoughts. I'd believe that there was someone else in the flat. I'd be so absolutely convinced of it that I'd start psychically preparing myself to be murdered. I'd lie there waiting for whoever it was to charge in and cut my stomach open with a huge knife, make gashes all down my arms and neck and generally do whatever else evil murderers do. Every little tick or creak became further proof that someone (a man) was there, outside my bedroom door, preparing to burst in. My whole body would start to tingle with a horrible kind of anticipation. It seemed so clearly to be about to happen that I couldn't stand the delay. The anxiety would set off all kinds of hideous chemical reactions in my body making me feel as though I'd been injected with bleach or blasted with lazers. It would get so painful I'd decide that, on balance, it would be better if he pounced sooner rather than later.

I think curiosity came into it too. I remember reading an article about that Japanese cannibal/novelist who ate a French girl. He went into amazingly graphic detail about carving up the human body. The bit that really grabbed me was the description of fat. Apparently human fat looks a lot like mashed sweetcorn. He described cutting into the girl's thighs and finding this lumpy yellow substance under the skin. I think it really struck me just because it was unexpected. I always imagine that my body is entirely red and bloody underneath, so the idea that there might be this strange yellow stuff just there below the surface really seemed thrilling. I love spots and blackheads – especially other people's – and all things that ooze and erupt out of bodies. If I see a big clogged pore I get a sort of sexual itch. I'm desperate to squeeze it and tweeze it and play with it.[1] It doesn't matter at all how undesirable the person is, I can actually feel my

[1]The MMM tells me this is a quality shared by all women. Is that true? Why do I feel so guilty about it?

mouth start to water and my heart speed up and I'm sure my pupils get all fat and leery. Once I pulled a lump of stuff out of my boyfriend's ear that was shaped like a champagne cork and actually popped. The idea of this sweetcorn fat grabbed me in much the same way. (I actually got to see it later in a film of a series of autopsies – a woman's body was split down the front and there it was, just like the article said it would be.)

Once I'd worked myself up into a frenzy of anticipation, waiting for my body to be shredded, any dread I felt would be combined with an overwhelming longing to see what it would be like. I'd actually get impatient. This looming presence in the hall who was waiting to chop me to bits was really taking his time. I'd be about to go to the kitchen to get a knife and do it myself (thighs first). The things that stopped me were:

1. The likelihood that I might not kill myself but just cover myself with scars and give myself serious medical problems.
2. The fact that I'd feel embarrassed in advance of when they found my body and it became apparent what a psychological mess I was.
3. The thought that if I stayed still enough the man in the hall might let himself out quietly and I might miraculously fall asleep and wake up a nice, normal girl again.

Next I'd have a big dilemma about whether or not to pull some clothes on and just get out. Then I'd get anxious about all the potential dangers on the streets at night. Finally I'd come to some sort of agreement with myself to leave the knives alone. But this arrangement could never quite be comfortably achieved as I felt that, even if I agreed that self-slaughter was a bad move, the man in the hall might burst in and do the job for me. Eventually I'd fall asleep when my brain couldn't be bothered any more and my body had exhausted its supply of adrenaline. But, after a couple of hours' rest, both head and body would feel refreshed and ready for a repeat performance. And so it would go on until it got light. Why am I telling you all this? Oh yes, I was just letting you know how horrible I was. In the midst of all these fantasies of self-mutilation, I'd suddenly find myself directing all my destructive energies towards my cat. If I couldn't hack myself to bits (for shame) I felt I could probably get away with doing it to him. (I'd just clean up the mess and say he disappeared.) He was really undeserving of such misdirected malice. I'd actually rescued him from a dustbin and the idea of saving him only to torture him to death seemed a little unfair. Admittedly he'd had some nice months in between (which is years in cat terms) so I might still have felt that I'd done him a favour. But I couldn't go through with it. I thought it might be a trap door to more hideous crimes. And I couldn't bear to think of how he'd react when he twigged to what was going on. He was one of those weird dog-like cats who really loves and trusts you and follows you to the shops. He and I had a lot in common – early abandonment leading to a gregarious nature with a propensity for obsessive love. So for the cat's sake I got a lodger who managed so successfully to defuse the situation (I'm not usually afraid when there's someone else there) that I felt instantly bored by my entire existence and moved within two weeks to a different city (with the cat).

This worked quite well for a whole three years. I lived in houses full of people and completely forgot about the man in the hall. But at the end of the three years I got into a university in London and had to return. At the same time, I fell in love and moved in with my boyfriend. I would have thought that having him around might prevent my morbid fantasies, but instead it made them worse. I started to worry that, not only would I hurt myself, but that I might hurt him too. I couldn't say anything because I thought it might frighten him off. But it was quite hard to explain some of the weird things I couldn't do – like go into our own kitchen. All this stuff had made its way so much to the surface of my thoughts that I couldn't pass the knife drawer without panicking about what might happen.

I didn't know how to deal with it, so I moved into another communal house and suggested that he go and live elsewhere. Meanwhile, I got myself a therapist and sorted out some of my stuff. Now we can live just the two of us together and I feel no urge whatsoever to stab him (mostly). And when he goes away I can sometimes even sleep on my own without leaving the radio on. I'm a walking advert for the power of psychotherapy. I guess the MA helped somehow too by turning my interest in blood and guts into a fully authorized academic activity. I could suddenly think all the gory thoughts I liked because the British Academy was paying me to do it.

⌐

I definitely don't have enough detachment from the people I love. I think it's a direct result of the postcard thing. I guess that on my first birthday I couldn't decide whether I was horrible, which had driven my parents away, or whether my parents were horrible for going away. I must have come to the conclusion that we were all equally awful – although it would have been a strange thought, not being formulated into neat little words, but all squelchy and baby-like and nebulous. I think my mind got stuck there, like it was pulling a gruesome face when the wind changed. When I like someone now, it reminds me how revolting I am, which makes me very anxious. I believe that, because I am so utterly rancid, they are very likely to leave me, which makes me hate them too. I'm a real Dennis Nielsen at heart. It's lucky my parents were nice to me after they got back from vacation or I'd definitely be a psycho already. Maybe this is why I feel such a strange bond with Philip. I'm the embryo to his fully fledged sociopath. I don't really believe that about him for a minute though. He's been very friendly since our lunch together and definitely doesn't seem like a murderer type to me.

I wonder how all my torment will reformulate itself in relation to the ∕∿∿∿. With luck my repressed violence is ceasing to be directed at myself and those I love and has moved onto bossy women in technicoloured crimplene. This seems to me a perfectly healthy resting place for it. The only drawback is that I will have to stick with the office manager if I want to have a happy romance. I think I am beginning to have a much deeper understanding of the would-be-fireman. (Although, if he ever actually became a fireman, perhaps he could start hating fires – and actually be allowed to kill them.)

12

Double Panic
(we meet again)

Anyway, to go back to where we were (rather a long time ago), after my first day at the Academy and our first night together – an evening of absolute romantic perfection (according to me) I waited TEN DAYS for the MMM's soothing phone call. It seemed impossible that he wouldn't ring, but then again he hadn't so far – and ten days was at least six too many. On the tenth day I got impatient (in fact I'd become impatient a couple of days earlier and tried to locate him by ringing anyone I could think of who knew him or might know him or have met him at least once, and failed to produce results). I think I finally decided that I was suffering too much as a result of the uncertainty of the whole thing and needed answers. Being told to piss off would be a huge improvement on this agonizingly drawn-out anxiety.[1]

By some miracle (the second so far) I found in my bag a scrunched up piece of paper with a picture, his name and some numbers on it. The numbers didn't appear to add up to anything like a phone number (hence the scrunchedness of the paper). I'd found it on the floor the day after the crying and kept it as a rather pathetic memento. The numbers looked more like a tax code or LEB customer reference. I guess it was their quantity and the

---

[1]By an amazing coincidence, someone at work is on the tenth day of a romantic telephone vigil. Because of what's happened to me since, I've been very encouraging. 'Ten days is nothing, it'll be okay,' I tell her blithely. How insensitive!

way they were spaced, but nothing about them suggested to me that they were in any way connected with the phone. However, ten days of romantic psychosis fuelled by starvation, thousands of cigarettes and a terrible new life persuaded me to take this scrap of rubbish to work with me and tap the numbers into my switchboard. It seemed as ridiculously optimistic as taking the bar code of my favourite chocolate wrapper and dialling it in the hope that the person who picked up and I would have a lot in common.

Unbelievably, this strange number produced a ringing tone, a result which I found so horrifying I hung up at once. Half an hour later, when the heart tremors had subsided, I dialled again and the phone was promptly answered by a very well-spoken man. I asked for the MMM, just to see what would happen, and was told by the well-spoken man that he was waiting for a call from him too, that he was holding too many screwdrivers to take a message and that maybe I'd bump into him first, in which case could I pass on a message myself? Who on earth could this annoying man with a stupid phone number be? I managed to bargain with him over the message-passing thing so that he eventually agreed to put his tools down and take my name and number. After hanging up the receiver I felt curiously appalled. I imagined that if the message got through at all it might take a couple of days. If he didn't call within the next week I decided it would be wise to assume that it was because he didn't want to. (But then how could he not want to? I was struck more than ever by the mysteries of relativity – how could we have had such different experiences of the same night?)

At about half past two that very same day he phoned. He seemed ebullient and full of himself and not at all at a loss for things to say. I mentioned maybe meeting and he said that either that day or the next were possible. I told him where I'd be later that evening and made a proper arrangement to see him the following night. I felt vertiginously euphoric for the rest of my working day.

That evening I went to where I was meant to go and met the friends I was meant to meet. We were late for the film we wanted to see and had to wait in the bar for the next screening. During the last few days my panic attacks had miraculously doubled so that now they happened at five o'clock too (like a second screening for those who couldn't make the first). The five o'clock ones were similarly narcoleptic, but at least once I'd left work I was allowed to pass out. When I met friends I'd just tell them I was very sleepy and have a quick lie down on a chair or sofa wherever we happened to be. Panic attacks are really common aren't they? At least I think they are, but they're like an unspoken Masonic type all-over-the-place-but-no-one's-actually-saying-so, open-secret, hand-tickling sort of thing. When you meet someone else who has them you communicate it to each other via semi-perceptible twitches and infinitesimally extended eye-contact and if they respond correctly you can just come right out and say it and instantly bond.

At the risk of betraying the brotherhood (and facing potential ostracism) I feel I ought to introduce the uninitiated to the mysteries of the panic attack. It's like being on the most powerful paranoia-inducing drug with no pleasurable side-effects whatsoever. You can feel yourself *being* to the most painful degree and would probably choose to stop if only you could think straight. However, suicide, like breathing, becomes such a crushingly complex notion that you can't even begin to contemplate it. You just have to wait for the panic to pass through your system and leave you in peace. I wonder if it's addictive. Panic attacks are about as normal as having flu or nosebleeds or bizarre taste in sandwich fillings. But when you're actually having one it seems like such a shameful, despicable thing. You feel like the most undesirable, useless, vile little toe-rag. And the last thing you want is to alert the world to your abject crappiness by telling them all about it (although, happily, one of your most impossible failings is your inability to articulate anything requiring more than two or three syllables, meaning that, even if you wanted to tell people how you were, you'd probably fail).

And that's how I felt, trying to sleep spread across two very uncomfortable plastic chairs underneath a plastic table while my friends (who'd never met) chatted overhead. Any minute now the MMM could walk in. I had to lose consciousness in order for there to be some small hope that I wouldn't embarrass myself completely. The one good thing about panic attacks though, is that, although you feel constantly on the verge of irretrievably shaming yourself, the likelihood is that you won't. While it may seem to you that everyone can see what a raving nut you are, they can't. Nonetheless I was convinced that if he walked in before the necessary moment of oblivion I might not be capable of preventing myself from burbling, foaming, contorting and perhaps even tearing at my face. Have you seen *Total Recall*? Remember the crazy woman at the spaceport who starts gibbering and splitting her head into neatly hovering cross sections (before she's revealed to be a sophisticated automated disguise designed to get Arnie through passport control)? Well, that sort of performance didn't seem at all out of the question if I didn't get at least thirty seconds' deep sleep. I must finally have passed out about fifteen minutes before the film was due to start and, as usual, woke up feeling stable, well-balanced and wholesome. I got upright, rearranged my bits and pieces and, the very moment my world had been restored to perfect orderliness, he walked in.

I don't really remember the picture I had formed of him during his absence, but the person who appeared in the bar wasn't quite the same as it. His hair was sticking up even more than usual and, underneath his scruffy suit jacket, he was wearing what looked like a blood-stained overall. On closer inspection the blood turned out to be paint, but either way it wasn't exactly pretty. His cheeks had sunken in a bit too, like he hadn't eaten much lately.

His perfect timing was only undermined by the fact that we

were due to go into the cinema in a couple of minutes. I'd waited ten days – going completely round the bend – to see him, and now I was going to have to rush off. (He'd already seen the film, I'd already bought my ticket and felt too awkward to say I'd prefer to see him.) Still, the quick exchange we had was pleasant enough – once I'd recovered from the shock of his appearance – and maybe the brevity of the meeting was quite a relief. We parted with a friendly 'see you tomorrow' type farewell and not even a kiss on the cheek.

The next day's plan was that I'd cook for him after dropping in on a drinks party. I was due to have the house to myself and, after seeing his sunken cheeks, I desperately wanted to feed him.

My happiness erupted uncontrollably as I made my way into the cinema. My friend (who's clearly more interested in hygiene than I am) just shrieked with laughter and commented on his 'dirtiness' – to which she clearly attached some erotic significance – and told me to make sure I used a condom.

When the film started I found I was affected by it to the point of discomfort. Even looking at colours was giving me excessive sensations. This thing I'm calling 'happiness' was becoming quite terrifying. I felt volcanic. But, as is often the way with these things, it proved completely unsustainable. About half an hour into the film it crumbled. The whole story of my stupid crush suddenly seemed preposterous to me. I wondered what it had been about. It evaporated. He was just an ordinary man, perhaps even quite horrible. I didn't want to meet him tomorrow, or ever. I don't really know what brought about the sudden change of heart – it just kind of happened before I felt I had a decisive role in it. It was really sad. I didn't feel relieved or pleased or like I might be saving myself some trouble. I just felt profoundly miserable. It was as if I'd lost the bit that had been holding everything together. My overblown romantic notions were perhaps the only thing in my life that were promising me any pleasure, and they'd gone. The situation was looking bleak, so I tried to let the film (an appropriate blend of violence, misery and nihilistic passion) do its work on me. Instead it sent me to sleep.

Just in time to catch the end, I woke up feeling chirpy and capable of getting back on with the love thing again. Sometimes I wonder whether I have a single rational electron floating around in my brain.

∽

I just had another lunch with Philip. This one was even better than the first. He'd been very friendly ever since, saying hello and walking past in a forwards direction, so when I saw him in the canteen today I decided to sit with him again. He looked really pleased for about the first three seconds and then he sort of crumbled. I couldn't imagine what was wrong and he isn't the sort of person you feel you can ask. It's as if by acknowledging that there might be something amiss you would be referring to everything not exactly right about him. I suspected that if I gave any hint things didn't seem altogether rosy he'd run off at once and probably knock the whole table over this time. He was really twitching, convulsing almost, and even when I asked him the most boring question – like whether his colleague's flu was getting better – he couldn't answer properly. He was muffling his speech more than usual, probably because the things he was saying made so little sense he wanted to obscure them. I really didn't get it. I felt like running off myself I found it so embarrassing. I certainly couldn't maintain my smugly calm position with him this time.

Luckily the pigeon lady walked in the door. I waved at her and she waved back and then joined the end of the food queue, which was unusually long. Philip and I carried on eating in silence for a few seconds but, remembering his previous reaction to a brief conversational lull I realized I had better say something or he might waste most of his lunch. In desperation I told him about an article I had just read on the uses of bastinadoes in ancient Rome. Miraculously, he calmed down at once. He asked me where I'd seen it and what it had said. I told him a few stories about slaves, spies and traitors being beaten on the soles of their feet and all at once we were friends again. The pigeon lady was getting nearer to the front of the queue, but now Philip and I had found something to chat about I was almost disappointed. I was right in the middle of a story about a 2000-year-old spiked truncheon that had recently been found in a bog near the back of my parents' house when she came and sat down. As she worries about pigeons with damaged feet I guessed she wouldn't want to eat lunch accompanied by a discussion of antique toe-crunching tricks. We both asked her if she'd had a haircut – which she clearly had – and then proceded to admire it. Three-way conversation ran out pretty quickly but, instead of getting embarrassed and rushing off, Philip got up at about average speed and said goodbye to us both before leaving.

The pigeon lady asked how on earth I had ended up next to Philip. I said that I was curious about him and she gave me a funny look. Maybe because she works upstairs and knows more about what he does all day she finds him less enigmatic than I do. I tried to explain why he seemed to me so utterly fascinating but she just didn't get it. She said as far as she could see he was just a very sad and lonely man. She's almost certainly not mistaken but I don't see why I should hold that against him. There's no reason why sad and lonely people should be any less interesting than people who are happy and sociable. In fact, in a lot of cases, the contrary turns out to be true.

It *is* quite funny the way he only looks happy when we talk about torture, but who am I to say that's wrong? The more I think about him the more I want to know him better. I'd love to know what he does in the evenings and what his house looks like. I doubt I'll ever find out though. It's as if there's a taboo around us becoming friends, like it would be pervy or somehow dishonourable. If I became close friends with the pigeon lady no one would bat an eye, just because she's female and we're around the same age. It's really unfair. I wonder how I could find out more about him. It seems so impossible to do it in the normal way that I have even considered the possibility of following him.

13

A Royal Visit

The King is coming to lunch at the Academy tomorrow. Well, not the King, but the Queen's husband. He is one of the patrons of the organization and is going to eat with the winners of an industrial design competition. What a funny job he has.

His Royal Highness's equerry has been coming for meetings, weeks in advance of the big day. Everyone here is going nuts about the visit – especially the office manager. Apparently, one of the main things the equerry has tried to make clear to her is that she needn't make a big fuss. What the Queen's husband likes most of all is to see people acting normally in their ordinary working environment. He doesn't like them to put on a show for him. He doesn't want his visit to upset anyone's professional routine. He's not afraid of seeing piles of paper and biros and all the bits of unaesthetic crap that form the material aspect of office life. When he goes out to lunch he is much more concerned about IRA bombs and kidnappers.

The equerry's job is to go ahead of the Queen's husband, calm everyone down, and make sure nothing terrible happens to His Royal Highness. Sniffer dogs have to come and check for explosives. Detectives have to come and assess the building's security programme – they look at the surveillance system, keep an eye out for undefended entry points and make sure that the receptionist is up to the task of keeping the bad guys out. I like to think that I would be, but I am a bit dozy sometimes. If a terrorist was polite enough, I'm sure he would be able to bluff his way past me. This responsibility scares me a little. I got this job because I thought it was the most inconsequential one available. Now I am in charge of making sure nothing nasty happens to the Queen's husband. I would hate to be partly to blame for his assassination.

The equerry is an amazing man. He is charming and handsome (in a weaslish way). The office manager goes weak at the knees when he comes to visit. It is his job to be polite to everyone – to grease the way for His Royal Highness's smooth entry. When he first came to the Academy, I didn't know who he was. He told me his name in a very clear, crisp voice and asked to see the office manager. I dialled her extension and realized that I had already forgotten what he was called. When I tried to apologize he completely disarmed me by apologizing back, telling me, in perfectly enunciated syllables, that it was his fault for being a mumbler. I was dazzled by his niceness – but is it really polite to lie in this unabashed way? I think it must be a quaint courtly perversion.

The ex-receptionist's reign of terror is drawing to a close. He has reached the end of his time at the Academy. The royal visit is to be the last thing he sees before he disappears. He and I will be at the door when the Queen's husband arrives. We have been told to wear suits and make an effort with our hair. I thought His Royal Highness was meant to love us as we were. Already the office manager is beginning to disobey the royal command. She is starting to try to cover over the fact that work takes place here, and to magic the office into a minimalist heaven where serious thought merely happens and is transmitted via telepathy. Files and work-trays have ceased to be considered functional objects and have become unacceptable eyesores. Post-it notes are banned. Rolls of sellotape are okay, but must be confined to drawers. I am worried that if we tidy up too immaculately the Queen's husband might believe that he was shot in the back in the doorway and is no longer a living body on the way to lunch with some engineers, but a soul passing through St

100

Peter's gates. I have stuck up a tiny photo of his wife to make sure he doesn't fall for this illusion.

Another funny thing that is going to happen when he comes is that, while he eats in the main room with the winners, the ex-receptionist, the would-be-fireman, the tea lady and I have been invited to eat in one of the smaller meeting rooms with the equerry, the royal photographer and two detectives. I don't know why we, rather than the accounts staff, or the membership people, or anyone else at the Academy, have been singled out for this treat, but I don't want to ask questions in case it makes them change their minds. Who decided it would be us? The equerry? The office manager? The director? Who knows. We will be eating the same food, drinking the same wine and being served by the same waitresses as the people in the main dining room while a rota of secretaries will kindly answer the telephone on my behalf.

～

At last, the big day has arrived. Everything is neat and nice, and everyone is apprehensive. The office manager is going crazy making finishing touches to everything. At midday she will knock off to make some finishing touches to herself. She has brought a special outfit. It scares me to think what this might be. Everyone has worn quite strange things today. It's interesting to see how they would like the Queen's husband to see them. The secretaries have almost universally gone for something floral. All the men are wearing their smartest suits and ties. Philip has, most surprisingly, gone for a yellow double-breasted jacket with gold buttons. The clever woman who probably knows about wood is wearing a very horrible, garish tartan suit with a white frilly shirt. The ex-receptionist is wearing a giant, baggy nineteen-forties suit and looks like a gangster. And I am wearing a fairly nasty pinstripe thing from Oxfam with a spotty tie. I also feel like I'm wearing

101

too much make-up. Why did I do this to myself? What's all the fuss about?

The only person who looks the same as usual is Heck. I've never really noticed exactly what he wears, but whatever it is, he's wearing it again today. Heck is in a very bad mood about the visit as he had to carry a heavy bucket of water upstairs for the plants. I think he may also be annoyed because he claims to be a prince, but is never given special treatment by the Academy. No one believes him. I believe him just because it seems to explain his fury at being forced to work. He hasn't even been invited to the rejects' dinner. When he came up with the water he was scowling more violently than usual. A very serious and bloody civil war has broken out in the country he is from. He said he couldn't understand why other countries weren't doing anything to help. Last night on the news it said the British and American governments didn't know what to do as they feared sending troops in might make matters worse. Three million people are about to starve – how bad do things have to get before they can't get any worse? Heck is a living reminder of what a fucking terrible place the world is.

However much I tidy up I can't seem to please the office manager. If I get rid of one set of problematic objects I just give the remaining ones more prominence. I guess I'll just have to keep going until it gets to twelve o'clock. I'd better put this away for a while . . .

. . . Well, that was boring, but at least I can stop clearing up now as the old bat has had to go home. In her extreme excitement she brought an odd pair of shoes for the occasion and has just raced off in a taxi. Perhaps I can persuade someone to fill in for me while I go and have a cigarette. Today is definitely making me tense.

It's twenty-five past twelve. He should be here in a few minutes. I can't really write much, but I just wanted to let you know what the office manager was wearing. I may find it hard to describe, though, as the trauma of seeing her really dressed up made her almost invisible to me. I think it was lilac, but it could have been peach. It had some crusty costume jewellery stuck on it. There may have been a ruffle. The shoes were almost definitely green. She had matching make-up. The horrifying part was that there was something almost pretty in her face. How has the royal visit made this woman pretty? Maybe there *is* something strange and magical about the monarchy.

The secretaries are all hanging out of their windows, waiting for a big car to appear. There is a giant policeman at the end of the street and a slightly smaller one just inside the doorway. The giant one has radioed to the smaller one to let him know that His Royal Highness ought to arrive in two minutes. The would-be-fireman is holding the door open. He will be the first person at the Academy to greet the royal visitor. The ex-receptionist is on the main reception chair, and I have been relegated to the position of vice receptionist. Even the ex-receptionist looks a bit awestruck (although, of course, he entirely disapproves of the existence of the Royal family). Everyone is breathless and jittery . . . I just heard on the walkie-talkie that the Queen's husband is on his way in. I'd better put this down . . . ✕ ♛ ✕ . . . That was one of the most fabulous disappointments I have ever suffered in my life. Not only did he not come by car – he just wandered down from the palace on foot – but he didn't stop to say hello to anyone. He was just a small, plain man accompanied by two larger men who walked in off the street and disappeared up the staircase. I only saw him from the back because no one realized it was him until he had gone past. Oh well, at least now we can go for our nice lunch.

⌐

Now I'm quite drunk, so I hope I can describe what our lunch was like. It had a sort of backstage feel about it. It was hard not to wonder what was happening at the real lunch next door. The detectives and the equerry kept going on about how much more fun it was to be in *our* room than *their* room. There was a vague idea that in their room everyone was restrained and boring, while in our room we could do and say whatever we liked. This didn't really seem to be true. We were all a bit tongue-tied and dull, while next door they were clapping and cheering from time to time and sounding quite lively.

In this new situation the equerry was tight-lipped and charmless. He asked us a bit about our jobs and we asked him a bit about his. He gave bland, noncommittal answers. He didn't seem to feel the need to be so charming when relegated to a table occupied by the Academy's low-life. The photographer was quite snotty too. It was as if he had become a royal photographer in order to give himself a bit of cachet, and was quite annoyed about the fact that he was cast aside at lunchtime to eat with the common people.

~

Why do social hierarchies kick in so effectively at mealtimes? What's the link between eating and reinforcing boundaries? Is it because mealtimes provide a perfect opportunity for verbal exchange? When you sit down to eat with people you have a good opportunity to find out more about who they are and what they think about things. And also to say some stuff yourself. What if, at lunchtime, the minion is more brilliant than the master? Who's in charge when you're just chatting? It's clearly possible to make rules about what can be said, and by whom, but this doesn't make for a relaxed atmosphere. Perhaps it's because you need to be relaxed in order to digest properly that people at different levels of the same hierarchy don't share mealtimes. If there are conversational legislations, then you can eat properly, but if there aren't, then the hierarchy might crumble.

104

People in powerful positions seem to have a need to retain as much mystique as possible. They are probably all haunted by the fact that it is only via a series of accidents and contingencies that they have ended up where they are. This, paired with the fact that people not in power-positions frequently harbour sadistic thoughts about those in charge and love to expose them as equals (even inferiors), means that eating together really could turn out to be a pain.

However, if people allowed themselves to suffer this pain they might bring about some very serious changes. The world might find it could no longer justify its differential treatment of people at varying social levels. The illusions that support these distinctions could no longer be sustained. The idea that some people were truly better than others would be repeatedly undermined. If more people ate together without feeling the necessity to be uptight and defensive, the world might become a fairer place. (I wonder whether my lunch with Philip has done any good in this way. I don't think so. When I had lunch with Philip I definitely felt like I was doing him as much of a favour as he was doing me. It seemed more like a fair exchange than a revolution.)

⌒

The ex-receptionist, after half a glass of wine, decided he was having none of this shit. He started to do what I believe was a parody of unrestrained behaviour. He dropped bits of lettuce onto my lap and picked them up with his teeth. He nicked bits of everyone's food. He asked the equerry what it was like to run around after 'that boring bastard' all day. He sang a bit. He asked the tea-lady to tell us all about her love-life. He found obscene shapes in all the food (a vagina in the salmon en croute, an arsehole in a small marzipan fruit) and asked the photographer to name them. He laughed uncontrollably at terrible jokes. And nobody knew quite how to react. It was spectacular. The equerry and the detectives excused themselves before the pudding. The photographer stayed, looking embarrassed, and left straight after.

The ex-receptionist and I stuffed the leftover bottles of wine under our jackets and finished them when we got back to the switchboard. Now I'm feeling a bit dodgy, but basically okay. I think royal visits are quite good.

~

Yesterday, when the Queen's husband came, they made him sign in a special book – not the one on reception. They gave him a whole page to himself and he signed it just with his Christian name. He ignored the ruled lines and wrote in big, childish letters.

14

Misery

Today I feel so miserable. I have a hangover, I'm not at all in the mood to pick up the phone, the ex-receptionist is no longer around, plus I haven't seen the MMM for a week and it's making me paranoid. I don't think he can like me very much. The last evening we spent together was another perfect one. He was at his most appealing and I was in an unshakeably good mood. We did romantic things like riding around on our bicycles in the dark and trying to kiss without putting the brakes on. We also went back to his warehouse and had extremely passionate sex – although afterwards it began to disturb me as I felt it may have been a little too ferocious. The sex we have is funny. I'm really far too embarrassed to describe it in detail, but I thought I should mention it as you probably suspect it must be quite good for me to be so nuts about him. You're right, in a way, and wrong in another. It's good in that it's quite wild and we make a lot of noise and knock things over and chuck each other round the room a bit. But where it isn't so good is afterwards. When we've finished doing all this really uninhibited stuff together, I go instantly back to feeling shy again and find that I can't possibly say all the things to him that I'd like to. I always imagine that once you've had sex with somebody you find that you can suddenly say anything to them. It never happens anyway, and it definitely isn't happening with the MMM. The sex is great but as soon as it's over I remember that I hardly know him at all.

The next day he left a rather terse message on my ansaphone

asking for a favour, and called me again at work to check that it was being done. The doubly insulting part was that the favour was something to do with material science and when he spoke to me it was only to get the name of the person at the Academy who could help him. This person just happened to be Philip and I felt incredibly irritated by the idea of them speaking to one another without me hearing. I do have the technology to eavesdrop, but I would be too afraid of sneezing and giving myself away. He was quite unfriendly, saying he wasn't ringing for a chat, so could I put him through quickly. It was such a vile call I wouldn't even give it the dignity of a ☎. He really made me feel like a receptionist.[1] And that's the last I've heard from him. (He still has one of my most precious possessions – my camera – so if he doesn't call soon I'll have to get it back somehow.)

To make things worse, the office has been filled with ridiculous miniature palm trees. They have been put here by some furniture designers who are using one of the conference rooms to launch their new collection. Here I sit, on the verge of tears, in the middle of an Agatha Christie theme party set. It's a freezing cold day and the front door has been wedged open to make way for passing sofas. Every time I think I've managed to hold back my tears, a huge, squashy, zebra-patterned monstrosity comes

---

[1] I found the best ever description of receptionists when I was reading *Remembrance of Things Past*. I try to think of it when I'm feeling bad about being one. Proust was being sarcastic, really, but if you cut off the last two clauses you'd never know. It comes just before the famous granny phone call so it gets a bit eclipsed. You have to be a receptionist to appreciate it fully. Anyhow, this is how it goes: '. . . the Vigilant Virgins to whose voices we listen every day without ever coming to know their faces, and who are our guardian angels in the dizzy realm of darkness whose portals they so jealously guard; the All-Powerful by whose intervention the absent rise up by our side, without our being permitted to set eyes on them; the Danaids of the unseen who incessantly empty and fill and transmit to one another the urns of sound . . .' Wow. It feels good to be appreciated. After that he turns into just another bastard who wants to slag receptionists off but up until then it's almost gushy.

hurtling past my face, making me feel queasy and morose. The furniture people are quite euphoric about this season's jungle designs and are unable to see that other people might not be quite so thrilled by them. They keep twittering and fluttering about like they're going to get married or go to the prince's ball. All they're doing is putting some ugly sofas in a room in the hope of exchanging them for cash. Why won't they go away and leave me to mope in peace? I wish the scary salesman would come and take them hostage or smash their kneecaps and extract some of their teeth.

Why is the ⋀⋀⋀ so bad about telephoning?

What makes me want to tell you all this garbage? It's so pointless. People go through this kind of stuff all the time and hate it and find it tedious and whinge about it to their friends or write a private diary or cry themselves to sleep every night and pretend to everyone around them that everything's okay. What on earth's the point of trying to turn all this swill into a novel? What are novels for anyway? I just started to read a contemporary American novel with a receptionist heroine (I thought I ought to check it out). It was like eating a box of assorted chocolates – all funny words and 'interesting' ways of saying things and witty (yet surprisingly 'deep') anecdotes and a plot that was really going places. I felt jealous and then I felt bored. But if you're looking for something that's really going all out to entertain I couldn't recommend it enough. (Although I've decided not to tell you what it is in case you take my recommendation seriously and abandon me.) See how I've turned this round? I feel terrible because I think I'm being solipsistic and dreary and not giving you what you want, but then there's this other person out there who seems to be doing all the things I claim to feel bad for not doing and I can't be scathing enough. His book sucks. He's so smarmy and such a writer. You can tell that he knows nothing about being a receptionist. I don't believe he even has any receptionist friends.

Why do I care? I'm just anxious about what it means to write a book and what books are and why people like them. The only reasons that are presenting themselves to me are ones to do with escapism and vicarious cleverness (whereby someone else does something clever and you think you must be clever because you understood it). *This* book dumps you right in the middle of a pile of things you'd probably rather not think about and perhaps doesn't seem particularly clever. But, as I know these aren't the only things that books can do (I'm just suffering a temporary amnesia), I won't give up yet. It's just that this potentially interminable cataloguing of the minor (to an outsider) ups and downs of amorous existence may have its limits. I'm looking for resolution and I can't see it anywhere. Not in life and not here. Perhaps people like books because they end. I feel like this thing with the ⋀⋁⋀ is about to end, but I don't like the feeling at all. Maybe it's a kind of girlie insecurity – I feel like I'm not foxy enough for him. Something about him makes me come over all schoolmistressy (and not even the good, bossy dominatrix type). He subdues me. I'm only half as good as he's there. Perhaps if I saw him any more than I do I'd grow to hate him. Maybe he's a terrible character and I just can't tell because I'm so acutely conscious of myself when he's around that I don't see him.

I promised myself I wouldn't ring him up and that I'd let him call me. But now I feel like calling him just to straighten out my head a bit. If we don't speak for a week I feel like he hates me. Am I making a fuss, or is it quite abnormal for people who ostensibly have feelings for each other to leave such long spaces between meetings? I'm actually a very busy person – I'm trying to keep the rest of my social life out of the picture as I don't want to offend *everyone* I know – so I'd just like to point out that if I want to meet the ⋀⋁⋀ I usually have to cancel something. I really do have drinks and films and parties to go to. I'm hardly bored between meetings, but having things to do doesn't stop me wanting to see him. What on earth can I possibly want from him? Why do I want to call him so much now? What do I get out of seeing him? Perhaps I could make it my mission to see what I can get out of not seeing him.

There is a Chinese proverb that says every minute a person makes you wait is a minute you will spend thinking about their bad points. The MMM may have quite a few unfortunate character traits but hardly enough to fill the days and days I spend waiting for him to call. I know I can always telephone him, but I don't want to be the one who does it every time. I don't want to think he only sees me because I oblige him to by calling. I want him to call me out of the blue, from choice.

I'll tell you what I think the problem might be. It's that the beginning of love is a story, the end of love is a story, but before the end the middle might mean anything. Perhaps it needs to be completed before it can be properly told. And here I am trying to tell it prematurely. I'm so impatient. All this not calling might have any number of explanations and outcomes, but until I know what's actually going on, it's quite meaningless. Or too meaningful actually to mean anything due to its infinite number of possible meanings. So shall I call him in the name of concluding an episode? Or shall I let it stay suspended and see what happens? It might be a big fuss about nothing, so perhaps I should take a couple of days off to read (and remember what books are for). ☎ (Just in case you thought I'd secretly started signing on or got a writer's grant.) Seems to me like a good idea to leave the MMM alone for a bit, change the subject etc. But, before we do, I'll leave you with this tremendous cliffhanger . . . (er . . .). After our brief meeting in the cinema I spent a truly horrible twenty-four hours with him which resulted in me proclaiming him to be loathsome and resolving never to see him again.

⌣

Oh no! I can't make myself not think about him. I want to call him now. I think I might tell the Academy that I want to leave. I'd really rather be an itinerant receptionist. Or maybe not a receptionist at all. I think I'd rather be a pop star or a teacher or an actress or a table-dancer. Maybe I'll start entering competitions with cash prizes. I need to learn to hustle and speak a foreign language. But first I feel the need to make a phone call. I imagine that if he told me to fuck off at this point it would be great. I'd be catapulted out into the world with nothing left to cling on to. Sex is probably very unhelpful at moments like this. It seems to prevent the necessary revolution. If I never had sex there's no way I'd tolerate this crappy job. Maybe I could get celibate for a while and see if it makes a difference to my career. Maybe I could try to sort things out a bit better with my boyfriend. Perhaps we could go to a marriage guidance counsellor. Not if she's like my Mum though. Despite the fact that it all seems to be falling apart, he has been very good company over the last few weeks. Since we noticed that we might genuinely be splitting up, we have started to appreciate each other a bit better. We haven't done any sexy stuff or anything, but we have definitely talked a lot about how we feel. The tragic truth, which I have been trying hard to ignore, is that I really do adore my boyfriend and feel pretty terrible about what I am doing to him. But the other side of it is that if I think about having sex with him I want to puke. I wonder whether a counsellor could fix this.

I still really want to call the MMM but the reasons are changing. Before, I think I was hoping that ringing might somehow give me something or kind of fill me up. But now I feel like calling might eject me into a life of unforeseen successes, dramatic events, incomparable riches, intense self-satisfaction, or a fulfilling adult relationship with the man I *really* love if only I could allow myself to recognize it. Three cheers for the telephone. MMM, please tell me to go away, because I can't

112

seem to do it of my own accord. It would be too abstemious – like giving up alcohol and coffee in the hope that it would make me a better person. I need not to be given a choice. I think I might even need to be rejected. Nothing's more guaranteed to increase my self-confidence. It's something I only fully realized recently and it's turned out to be a very handy thing to know. If people tell you that you're lovely, beautiful, intelligent and talented, then all you can think is that you've somehow managed to put something over on them, and you pray that they won't twig. If people tell you that you're not quite what they're looking for, difficult, inappropriate, wrong, they're ninety per cent guaranteed to make you feel brilliant, incandescent, a genius, a star. Of course they don't understand your unique brand of superiority. How could they? They're ordinary. So all I need from the МММ is just such an igniting rejection. (How strange to need someone to teach you that you don't need them.) ✍!

⤳

The most incredible messenger just came in with a package. Most bike messengers are quite incredible – including the МММ – but this one was really noteworthy. He had even more facial piercings than all the others put together. He was dressed in black, but he made it look even more black than the black stuff the average courier wears. He was made from a huge amount of muscle coated in a huge amount of fat. It was freezing outside but he was wearing a tee-shirt which showed off the tatoos on his arms. I might have imagined it, but when he opened the door it was as if some dry ice came in with him. He slammed the package down on the desk and thrust his biro at me, clicking it into the operative position like a flick knife. I was so impressed with his entrance that I signed the delivery form without looking at the label. Just after he stormed out I realized that the name on the package – Sir L. L. Lippoch – didn't match anyone working at

the Academy. The address was correct though. Bollocks. I hate
having to deal with annoying crap like this. I have much better
annoying crap of my own to sort out. I didn't even catch the
name of his courier company.

~

I have a photograph of the ∧∧∧∧ in front of me. The more I
change my mind about things the more it changes. He's standing in a park in a tartan beret with his hand on his hip pulling a
kind of Popeye face, with his lower jaw jutting and his forehead
wrinkled, his eyes squinting and a look of being on the verge of
laughter. His laugh lines are really pronounced and his fingers
seem to be about to slide into his pocket. It's super-sexy. When
I got it back from the chemist it made blood rush to my head.
The first time they processed the film they skipped that picture
by mistake. I only discovered it when the negatives fell on the
floor and I held them up to see whether they had any crap on
them. When I got it printed it seemed like it was special because
it had been a sort of secret, hiding out in the packet for a while.
I may have been a bit superstitious about it, but I felt as though
it got missed the first time because it had accidentally managed
to get too much of him in it. It looked almost indecent. It was
so full of him that I was in danger of being in love with *it*,
completely forgetting that it was just a little rectangle of paper.
It was weird. It's incredible how mixed up I can get about which
bit of the ∧∧∧∧ I am claiming to be in love with. I wonder
if someone were to have plastic surgery to make themselves
identical to the photograph I would go mad about them too.
What if my boyfriend did? Would I suddenly find him sexy? I
think I can say for a fact that I wouldn't be impressed.

Right now it just looks like a picture of a strange and ugly
man. (Still, I'm quite a fan of ugliness.) What would it look
like if I spoke to him?

* * *

I just rang and he was out.

The picture looks tragic to me now. I'm more than certain that he doesn't like me at all. And during my lunch hour it occurred to me that I'm not even slightly pleased but actually feel quite upset and unconfident and brimming with self-hate. This certainly isn't what I like. I actually think I'd like to be loved and happy – strangely enough.

15

Acting

I used to live in a small cul-de-sac in a small city next to two
small children who'd come to play in my house all the time.
They'd dress up in my clothes, my jewellery and my make-up
and then charge around, tripping on my hems, falling off my
shoes and smearing my lipstick all over their faces. When they'd
tired themselves out they'd get miserable because their parents
were separating and they wanted to speak to their dad. Their
mum wouldn't let them call him from their place, so they'd try
to call from mine. If I made an attempt to stop them they'd go
berserk. I couldn't stand seeing them so distraught so I'd give in
and let them ring. They'd dial and speak to their father, handing
the receiver back and forth between them. When they felt they'd
said enough, they'd hang up, apparently feeling much better,
and we'd carry on the game. This would happen a couple of
times a week and I started to worry about their mother (who
thoroughly disapproved of me but didn't object to the free
baby-sitting service) finding out and getting angry. I thought
perhaps I ought to supervise the calls to make sure they weren't
planning anything she wouldn't like. I'd watch them dial and
slowly it dawned on me that the numbers were always different
and that they never dialled the full quota of digits. Nevertheless
the 'conversation' would take place and peace and happiness
would be restored.

Maybe this is something I ought to try.

16

Dialogue

'Hello...hello...is that you?.........Well that's good 'cos it's me. How's things?....... Oh really?.......................That sounds exciting...Really?...... Brilliant. Good for you.......................Mm.......................Mm ....Mm .... You must be so pleased ....
.... yes, that's excellent news.. Me? Well, not much really...well, quite a lot actually, but nothing really to tell stories about, doing stuff but I can't really remember what or why. So tell me more about this thing you're doing
....
....
....
..........................Yeah?...
.............Oh my God! You're so lucky....Well, not lucky........
....................................You know what I'm trying to say......
.............................Anyway, it's a really good bit of news and I'm happy for you ....What? You're waiting for a call from them right now?............Oh gosh then, I'd better go. Well, bye. It'd be nice to see you one time. Yeah. Bye.'

Well, that was a pretty unsatisfactory attempt. Try again.

'Hello...............Yes, it's me.........................Oh, that's very nice of

you.......................................Yes...
..Mm...............................Mmmmmmmmmmmmmmm........
....Oh, I'm fine. Well I am now...
.....................Really? Would you like that?.................yes.....
...............................Mmm....................Oh!.................Any-
way, how are you?..............................Ohwow!.......................
......................Oh stop! You're too much sometimes..............
......................I'm going to have to...........Oh my God. I'm on
the floor.................Oh yes...........................What with the
receiver? Wow! But then we won't be able to talk....................
....You don't mind.................You'd
like   that?.............Mmm.......................Oh........................
.................Oh....................Ohhhhh.................................
....yes.......aaaarghhhh[plus panting
noises]................................... Oh!.................Ooohhhh [five
minutes pass in this way]........................ Are you still there?.....
....
....Oh baby, can we just lie
like this?.....We don't have to talk..
....
....
....
. . . .
. . . .
. . . . . .

. . . . . . [Some kissing sounds] . . . .

. . . .

. . . .

Goodnight.'
Click.

17

An Educational Interlude

What would Alexander Graham Bell think if he knew how vital his invention had become in the field of romantic relations? Almost all kinds of human relations, in fact. The phone has got itself mixed up right in the middle of everything. It can sometimes seem like the actual handset is as important as the people who use it. I wonder how many telephones have been thrown at walls for delivering the wrong information (or no information at all).

I can't imagine life before the phone. I almost don't believe in it. Everything must have been so slow and such a hassle. The history of the world should be renumbered starting at zero on the day we now call 2nd June 1875, when Bell's assistant, Watson, twanged a metal strip in such a way as to accidentally produce a sound in Bell's receiver.

Certain people had known for ages that phones, or something like them, would be invented. A highly trustworthy prophetess is said to have predicted the birth of the telephone with the following phrase: *Around the world words will fly in the twinkling of an eye*. It's not exactly specific, but the fact that she felt it and that other people remembered is surely a sign they could all see it was a good idea and were keen for it to happen. You probably already know that the phone was simultaneously invented by two different people: a man called Elisha Gray arrived at the Patent Office only two hours later than Alexander Graham Bell. Apparently Gray's plans were much better elaborated than Bell's, but Bell had made a prototype that actually worked so they let him have the patent. You might argue that the phone so obviously had to be invented it's hardly surprising two people thought of it at once. Or you might say it was merely a simple step up after the invention of the telegram. But apparently the most likely explanation is that both of them cheated. I got a book about it from the library once. I think it meant a lot to me because my of dad's work. Inventors are the real heroes of modern life, and they mostly have quite a tough time. My dad gets completely crazy about it. One of the things that upsets him more than almost anything else in life is that the man who invented the reflective cats' eyes that run down the middle of most major roads in the world didn't patent his idea. He would probably have been one of the richest people ever but he missed out due to a legal oversight. If you ever go driving at night-time with my father he gets really melancholic about it. The business of inventing is full of pitfalls like this. There was an inventor called Antonio Meucci who had, according to a large number of witnesses, built a rather ungainly talking-gadget for use around his house. In 1871, five years before Bell's patent was granted, he was involved in a serious ferry accident between Staten Island and New York. His disabled wife couldn't support him while he recovered and sold his talking-gadget to a junk dealer for five dollars. They were so broke, even after he got better, he couldn't afford to make a new one.

The gadget had been very useful around the house (particularly with the wife being immobile) and Meucci felt sure he should somehow be able make money out of his invention – if only he could raise enough cash to get started. He approached various sponsors, but people either didn't believe it was possible, or didn't think it was such a brilliant idea anyway. (You have to appreciate that, in those days, no one had ever heard a voice coming out of anything other than a mouth and it took some effort for them to be able to deal with the notion without feeling deeply unsettled. They were obviously expecting the prophecy to come true in some other form.) In desperation he got a caveat for his invention, went to the American District Telegraph Company with a huge folder of details explaining how the thing worked, and asked whether he could test it on their lines. The people in the office were unconvinced and refused to co-operate. They passed the folder onto a couple of electricians at a company called the Western Union. The electricians failed to understand the notes and lost them somewhere down the back of a desk. Meanwhile Mr and Mrs Meucci stayed home and carried on starving. (This last bit has just reminded me that Sir L. L. Lippoch's package has been sitting on my desk for a few days now. I must do something about it. I have asked a few people as they walked past if the name means anything to them but nobody seems to know or care.)

A couple of years later both Elisha Gray and Alexander Graham Bell began using the Western Union lines to test the results of their experiments. They had far better financial backing than Meucci and finally persuaded the company that 'talking telegrams' were a catchy idea. (Bell was engaged to the daughter of one of the richest men in America and had to make his own fortune somehow before the marriage could go ahead. Luckily his future father-in-law approved of him and gave him a helping hand.) When they arrived at the Western Union, neither Bell nor Gray had yet got the hang of making a voice come out at the other end of a line. Luckily, they found themselves assisted by the exact same technicians who had seen Meucci's folder.

Gray and Bell were in hot competition with one another. Bell in particular was paranoid about Gray nicking his ideas. There is a really terrible nineteen-forties' Hollywood version of this part of the story, which you might get to see if you ever catch flu. The whole drama centres around the sanctity of Bell's genius – Gray is definitely the bad guy. The bit they leave out of the film, but which is almost certainly what happened, is the part when the evil Gray and St Bell chat with the technicians about Meucci's incomprehensible notes. What had made little sense to the electricians would have meant quite a lot to Bell and Gray, who had been working on the idea for a few years. Which might explain how come they both had their eureka moments at much the same time. The diaphragm and vibrating metal strip technique of transmitting speech, 'discovered' simultaneously by Bell and Gray, was exactly the one used by Meucci in his original talking-gadget.

Meucci went mad when he found out that someone else was getting all the credit for something he'd done more than five years earlier. He took the case to court (as did about four hundred other people who also claimed to have invented the telephone first). He managed to get the folder back from the Western Union and produced countless witnesses, including the junkshop owner who had bought and sold the device. It was pretty obvious to the people at the trial that Meucci had a point. The problem was that the American Bell Telephone Company was already one of the biggest businesses in the country. If the judge had admitted that Meucci's caveat was enough to invalidate Bell's patent then it would apparently have had a serious affect on the American economy. The judge probably didn't want to be responsible for making such a mess (there is nothing to suggest that he was bribed) so he allowed the rich corporation to win the case, hoping that Meucci could be passed off as yet another fraudster trying to cash in on Bell's success.

Meucci tried endlessly to appeal, without any luck. He died in abject povery in 1889, still insisting to anyone who would listen to him, that he was the inventor of the telephone.

The whole thing is so sad. But the thing I find saddest of all is when I think that Bell, Gray and Meucci were just three dreary engineers of the sort I have to meet every day. I wonder whether any of the old codgers who come to the Academy are working on an invention that will revolutionize the way human beings relate to the world and to each other. When you watch the way they bumble around it doesn't seem remotely possible. But I will certainly make an effort to trace the owner of that package, just in case. I'll try to be more efficient with the messages too, although I do find it implausible to think that by mentioning one silly name to another silly voice I might be able to speed up the process of global technologization.

18

I Hate Work
but Love Lunch

I love lunch. My lunch hours are always beautiful. Not simply because my job is in one of the most beautiful parts of town, it's just that I really do forget work for an hour and get into smoking and eating. I have boycotted the staff canteen and now spend the entire sixty minutes imagining myself an autonomous, uninstitutionalized entity. (I love food again – so this must be a serious romance. Not eating is for the merely infatuated.)

I'm also impressed by the sublime regularity of it. The time and duration of my outing are as if decreed by the unimpeachable Lunch God. He sends down his angels (Tara, Karen, Sherry and Elise) to relieve me of the burdensome duty of receiving calls. I am released into the city to eat and smoke myself back to happiness.

At the beginning of the hour the kindly God smiles on beleaguered telephonists, but at two o'clock he turns malevolent and can only be placated by the return of the sorrowful workers to their toil.

It's five to one and the Lunch God is happy. Tara is being spirited down by the lift and I will eat pizza or sushi or sandwiches and cake.

The only downside of these free-form lunches is that I now have even less hope of ever coming to understand Philip. I do still talk to him in the tea room whenever I get the chance. But now I would actively *like* to meet him more often he hardly ever seems to be there. You can't talk that much in the time it takes to boil a kettle anyway, but it's always nice. Even though we just talk about nothing much, it's as if we have a special understanding. He's still jumpy and weird, but I guess if you've been that way for fifty or so years you're not going to change your whole personality just because your receptionist starts being nice to you. It makes me happy to see Philip relax a bit. I feel like a zoologist who has managed to befriend a particularly timid wild animal. Whereas I used to think of him as a baked bean, now I think of him more as a gazelle or something. I'd love to be able to study him better in his natural habitat. But maybe the Academy *is* his natural habitat. He's always here when I arrive and leaves after I do. I would like to imagine that he has this fantastic secret life elsewhere, but maybe it's true that he just comes here, works really hard, and then goes home late and goes to sleep. But if that's the case, what has he got to be so nervous about? There's clearly a lot going on underneath that boring bastard veneer – even if it *is* only in his imagination.

19

24 Hours

Since promising to tell the story of the disastrous twenty-four hour date – our first meeting since the ten day wait (apart from the cinema one, which didn't really count) – I have done just about everything I could to avoid thinking or talking about it. After a reasonably nice phone call from the MMM, not to mention a quick visit this morning at the Academy (in tight shorts and walkie-talkie) I feel almost ready to allow myself to remember what happened. It was horrible. I'd spent the entire daytime dreading it. I was scared to death. What if I flipped? What did I want? What if he turned out to be awful? What if my entire romantic fantasy fell apart tonight? I couldn't imagine having anything to say. I'd had the odd daydream where I was lying in his lap and telling him everything, but I kind of guessed it wouldn't happen.

Between finishing work and meeting him I tried to have a nap. I tried park benches, grass, stairways, cafés, the tube, but sleep was not forthcoming. I tried to soothe my troubled head with healthy and refreshing soft drinks. But the fact soon had to be faced that I felt like a stark, raving loon and there was very little I could do about it. I could always not turn up, but I figured this course of action would exacerbate the problem in the long run. It also occured to me that seeing him might be the remedy I was looking for, and that the moment he materialized I could wave my nervous symptoms goodbye. This rather ludicrous bit of romantic optimism made me feel less gloomy and strengthened my resolve to go and face him.

I arrived at the designated meeting-spot about ten minutes

early and tried to calm myself down by toying with the notion that the world was a delightful place. It didn't really work.

For some mysterious reason we had arranged to meet at one of London's busiest pedestrian junctions at the height of the rush hour. There were people swarming all over the place. And peppered through this morass of highly motivated directional movement were a number of less efficient looking drunks, one of whom told me he could see my knickers – which, given the nature of my outfit, couldn't possibly have been true. Nevertheless he went on to give a fairly accurate description of them. Amazing.

Ten minutes later the /\/\/\/\ appeared. He had on the same splattered shirt as the night before, only this time with a pair of gory trousers to match. (I wonder whether anyone else in the world has an outfit like this. It may be the feature that finally gives him away. If you ever see anyone in a blood-suit you can be almost certain it's him. It was just such an outstanding detail that I feel it would be almost indecent to ignore it.) I was wearing a sparkly dress and was clearly dressed for a date. I felt a bit ridiculous. We said hello awkwardly but nicely and turned in the direction that we needed to go. He stopped suddenly, picked me up and swung me about a bit, which was good of him. I couldn't quite show how much I secretly appreciated this gesture as I suddenly felt myself inexplicably transformed into a kind of prim elder sister character in the style of Jane Austen.[1] This nonsensical 'suddenly I found myself . . .' style turn of events really took me by surprise. I mean we're still talking reality (I'm not going to claim that my dress too became a sprigged and frilly cotton pinafore with bonnet)

[1] I'm obsessed with Jane Austen, I think. I never really noticed until now. I like to believe we have a lot in common. She wrote quite secretively on single scraps of notepaper, while I write slyly on the dilapidated old computer in semi-retirement on my reception desk (switching to a grey notepad when I'm out of the office). She was also interrupted constantly by people inviting either themselves or her to tea. Imagine if *Sense and Sensibility* had a little ✉ (it's a calling card – I couldn't find a teacup) to show how frequently social calls came between poor Jane and her writing.

but only just. This was the last thing I expected. If I'd had to turn into someone else I would at least have predicted more of a crazy Mrs Rochester type. But this kind of Elinor Dashwood was a semi-pleasant surprise (her main literary *raison d'être* being her profound good sense). Enough. We had to go to this drinks thing before I got to cook, but first we went for a walk followed by a pint (very un-Elinor). The sleep problem was hitting me really hard, so I decided it was best to let him know that at some point – maybe in the pub – I was really going to have to pass out. He didn't take my request at all seriously (but then why should he?) and began to talk more and more animatedly about himself, his work, his situation, his problems, to the point where I really wondered what on earth I was there for. He barely seemed to be addressing his speech to a person. He was still trying to decide whether or not to leave the country, which involved trying to work out ways to earn money. Because he didn't know what he was doing he had allowed himself to become homeless – hence the number on the scrunched up paper being the only means of contacting him. Basically, he was in a big mess. I found it difficult to know quite how to deal with this new state of affairs. He just didn't appear to be at all whoever he'd seemed to be before (I'm going to have to add a symbol for when I'm interrupted by a person at work asking whether I'm writing my memoirs or a love letter: ♥). If I'd gone all Elinor Dashwood, he'd gone malconnected-android-speed-freak-solipsist. It was like he'd got so wound up about his life he'd given up on the idea of being able to relate to people any more. After the pint I was quite relieved to be able to go and join my friends at the party. Luckily there was someone he knew there, so I lost him at the door.

This was one of those occasions where you go to a party not really knowing who'll be there and it turns out that you know all of them. On seeing this particular selection of people I know, I felt quite relieved. Although I do remember getting quite panicky again and trying to go for a quick nap in the loo (which turned out to be far too uncomfortable).

There was a story going round about a man we all knew beating up a woman we all knew. Everyone became very moral and melodramatic when they talked about it and it made me feel nauseous. I liked both the man and the woman, although I didn't know either well. But I hated the way we couldn't stop talking about them. We didn't even have anything interesting to say. Being part of a group can make you such an idiot. You just drop all your intricate thoughts and reactions in order to be able to say 'How horrible!' alongside everyone else.

When the drinks ran out everyone went to the pub. At this point my friends turned into cumbersome menaces. They sat around ruining the last shreds of hope I had for my date, disapproving of the MMM and trying to make me hang around for ever, messing everything up and preventing me from cooking. They seemed to find him as strange and hard to deal with as I did, with the vital difference that they weren't trying to be in love with him. Unlike me they could just allow themselves to find his glazed manner and tiresome monologues annoying. My friends can sometimes get a bit protective and they made it quite clear that they thought the MMM was bad news. I was feeling very down on group mentality, though, so I decided to ignore them.

While earlier I'd felt like the MMM was trying to avoid me (thanks to my newfound prissiness) now he began to disturb me by being constantly at my side (perhaps he was getting a bit hungry). I didn't feel like we were getting on at all well. It was as if this anything-goes-love-fantasy had become so utterly desirable to me that anything less was a catastrophe. I didn't feel even slightly close to him, but how close would be close enough? Stupidly, I blamed him for whatever unavoidable chasm there was between us – I felt he was putting it there out of malice. Eleven days before he had been cuddling and stroking and singing me songs and now he was acting like the Lawnmower Man. He must have noticed the difference too. I was in a real temper – but not the sort that anyone else could notice. I gave up on the cooking idea altogether and decided I felt like going to a restaurant. This story takes place in London, however, which means that, if you go for a few drinks in the first part of the evening, everything will be closed by the time you get hungry.

It was a freezing cold night and it might have been drizzling a bit too. Walking down a side street towards one of the last possible restaurants in town, he pressed me face-first into a shop window, squashing me with his entire weight and biting me hard all over the back of my neck. Suddenly I felt considerably better. The ⋀⋀⋀ is very intelligent in this way. Just when you're thinking he's a bit cut off and getting lost somewhere inside himself he turns round and does exactly the thing that you'd most like him to do. I always wanted a telepathic boyfriend and when the ⋀⋀⋀ does stuff like that I get really excited. I suppose I'm just desperate to be understood. I thought a telepathic person would be great because they'd be used to all the dodgy things that everybody thinks about and would be very accepting. They'd also be able to get down to all the stuff it's difficult to say, without you having to agonize about whether or not to say it. Maybe the ⋀⋀⋀ *is* telepathic which is why he has such a funny manner (and why he seemed to understand why I was crying so much that day). What a crap theory. Next I'll be telling you about how I always wanted to have a tiny boyfriend that I could carry around in my pocket.

We decided to go home to eat and began the long wait in the cold for a night bus. When the bus didn't come we wandered off into the park and into a pile of deckchairs. I don't want to describe the ensuing sex too graphically but, to give you some idea of what it was like, try to imagine the very controlled rape fantasies that some women reputedly have (they're being raped but they're not in any real danger so they just let themselves get into it (according to News of the World this is the second most popular fantasy after the football team one (who on earth did they interview?))). It was quite rough and I had sore patches

131

on my face and body for a few days afterwards. I think I did sort of enjoy it, but in the way that you might enjoy a big steak if you hadn't eaten for a few days. At first you'd just want to wolf it down, but about three-quarters of the way through you might start feeling a bit off. A couple of people walked quite close by while it was happening and we didn't even stop. After our first, condom-free night of passion it was really a bit of a shock. I had hoped for more singing and cuddling and certainly hadn't bargained on a quick public shag and a bruise on the head from a chair leg.

Straight afterwards, we gathered all our bits together, walked up towards the Ritz and jumped into a taxi. It must have been one o'clock when we got to my house. I had failed to go to the supermarket, so all I could offer him was oven chips. Another drama, more serious than the food, was that my boyfriend – who had gone to a party on the other side of London – might have made up his mind to stay out, or might have decided to come home. I had really mismanaged the whole affair. The МММ and I were meant to come home earlier, but he had freaked me out so much that I hadn't been exactly desperate to get him on his own. Then I was supposed to cook him an amazing dinner during which we were meant to talk deeply and truthfully about everything. After that we were supposed to go to bed and tenderly make love. And then, understanding my tragic set up, he was supposed to leave before the boyfriend came home. It's lucky I'm not a prophetess as I would be no good at the job.

The thought of my boyfriend's potential return made me so anxious I double locked the door in the rather feeble hope that I might be able to prevent it. I imagined he'd hate to meet the МММ, and that the МММ would be rather surprised to meet him. The boyfriend was aware of the МММ's existence, but didn't necessarily want to come home to find me in bed with him. We hadn't discussed the arrangement with our flat at that stage, but I guessed a faux pas like this could speed up the whole process. Because the boyfriend and I had failed to address our problems, I hadn't told the ΛΛΛ that we might be separating, as it wasn't that simple. The truth was that we didn't know what we were doing. I'd have loved to have been able to talk about stuff like this with the ΛΛΛ, but didn't quite know how to go about it. He asked so few questions that evening I assumed he didn't want to know too much about my life.

After the chips he and I went to bed in the spare room and jumped on each other only slightly more tenderly than before. A few minutes into this slightly brutal scene there was a clinking of keys at the door followed by an incessant ringing at the doorbell. I felt instantly cold, shaky and petrified. I had no idea how to behave or what to do. I told the ΛΛΛ who it was and said that I didn't think it would be a good idea to let him in. My boyfriend is extremely mild mannered and gentle and part of the reason I didn't want to let him in was that I couldn't face seeing this delicate, polite person confronted by a situation where delicacy and politeness had so far found no place. It would have been like an alien invasion. I couldn't imagine how either he or the ΛΛΛ would deal with it. It's true that maybe we could all have sat down together and talked it through, but to me, at the time, this seemed absolutely out of the question. What was going on between the ΛΛΛ and me was hardly mature behaviour, so why pretend the situation could be brought under control by a measly performance of grown-up conduct?[1]

The doorbell kept ringing and we carried on having sex. The ΛΛΛ, knowing nothing about the boyfriend, was under the impression that his life might be in danger. In his imagination

[1] I actually feel very deep regret about not having done the thing I'm presently justifying not doing. I really do miss some opportunities to behave like the kind of person I wish I was. I'd like to take this chance to say sorry to my boyfriend, sorry to the ΛΛΛ, and a small apology to myself and whoever else is listening.

it apparently seemed that this rather effete man on the other side of the door was a gigantic, hairy, ferocious brute. Now, it seems so stupid of me not to have taken the situation in hand, but I felt totally incapable. I was in the middle of having sex with someone who'd driven me completely insane with longing and then re-appeared in new (and far less appealing) form, and I couldn't just switch the whole situation off and start behaving like a reasonable person. And anyhow, if the ∧∧∧∧ had wanted to know about my boyfriend he could always have asked.

The doorbell eventually wore itself out into a sort of sickly rasp. Without the clamour of the bell to distract him – and in spite of his mortal terror – the ∧∧∧∧ became more masterful in bed, flinging my legs into the air and getting back into being a bit more cocky and obnoxious. Afterwards, I hurried him back into his clothes and suggested that he sit quietly in the spare room, even try to sleep, and slip out when the boyfriend was tucked up in bed. This plan seemed feasible (despite its rather farcical nature – the nature of farce being to show plans like this tragically (comically) failing).

I went to open the door but my boyfriend was no longer there. I waited and called out but he didn't appear, so I gave it a few minutes and then went back to the spare room to sleep next to the ∧∧∧∧. He kept his clothes on and we lay on opposite sides of the bed.

I guessed I was about to be made homeless. And deservedly so.

The ∧∧∧∧ and I had a plan to do something the next day which involved waking up very early. ♥ We leaped up at half past seven after a paltry amount of sleep and began our long day taking photographs of different parts of London. The morning was nice enough and it was almost as if last night hadn't happened. We didn't mention it once.

We went to Hyde Park, Waterloo, the British Museum and around the backstreets near Holborn. We chatted (or at least *he* did) but it was hardly the emotional deluge I was hoping for. I'm sure it was no more boring than plenty of other conversations I've enjoyed in the past, but it didn't nearly match up to my hopes, reducing what should have been okay to something horribly empty and flat.

By midday I was absolutely exhausted. I'd been trying to get some sleep since five o'clock the day before and I'd only got a couple of hours in before starting all over again. After a brief spell of morning enthusiasm I was ready to collapse. My exhaustion was beginning to make me morose. I started to feel embarrassed about being so dismal in front of him – I just couldn't keep up any more. By about one o'clock I'd had enough and really needed to get some proper rest. I felt the sort of loss of equilibrium and self-control you might feel after being kept up in a police cell all night in preparation for an interrogation. (Strange, however, that I should find myself making this analogy, because I think the thing I wanted most of all was a bit of interrogation from him.) I decided to make a break and get myself back to normal. I said goodby to him quite suddenly and turned into a shop (!). Amazingly, despite all the difficulties and dramas of the night before and the slightly tiresome morning, I still suffered the universal evanescing experience. We hadn't exactly had a great time together but his disappearance could still hollow out solid objects, alienate me from my fellow beings and radically alter the texture of my entire perception. Time went funny. Suddenly its passing became incredibly painful – almost as if it was much too slow, even though I could see that all the buses and the people were moving at their familiar speed. The nearest thing I can relate it to in everyday life is the feeling you get when you're on a long train journey and are unbearably impatient to arrive. You go crazy with frustration but are completely powerless to do anything about it. The more desperate you become to get to where you're going, the more you start realizing that, even when you arrive at the station, you'll have to get in a car and go somewhere else. Even when you reach your *next* destination, you'll have things to do, like

135

change your clothes to go out to dinner. You realize that you're never going to arrive permanently *anywhere* and that the rest of your life will be as unsatisfying as it is for you right now.

This time I really couldn't stand it. It was horrible enough the first time, but twice in two weeks was at least once too many. I had to find the MMM as, in my state of apocalyptic meaninglessness, I felt I might easily damage myself by mistake. Or even on purpose. Bodily pain can occasionally announce itself to me as a possible route back to normality. I imagine that if I cut myself deeply enough it might be a quick way to reintroduce myself to the realities of my body and thus to the realities of other bodies and things. I was stuck in the middle of ☎☎☎☎☎ (Oh no, I've started noticing again) one of the busiest streets in London, desperate to find the MMM before I was compelled to open some flesh. I thought a crash might be good too (although I'd have less control over the damage and might wreck my face – not to mention the fact that I was wearing a distinctly un-crash-friendly outfit) just because it would mean that my being would instantly be passed into the care of others. I'd lose responsibility for myself for a while. I think this is perhaps all I wanted but, at that time, I wanted most of all to be taken care of by the MMM. One of the very good things about the MMM, however, is that he is largely unprepared to provide this sort of service. It isn't that he's uncaring (well, it is sometimes), it's more that he seems to understand that you need to be able to look after yourself before you can go around asking other people to help you out. I'm right with him on this one, but perhaps I give the impression of being someone who isn't. I think I have the manner of a person who needs looking after – and so I often meet people who are prepared to give it a go. Unhappily for them though – thanks to the perversity and general contrariness of human nature – I always grow to despise them. I can't stand to be looked after by someone who thinks they're in love with me. It makes me sick to see people turn pathetic and servile in relation to my demands. What's got me onto this one? I think I just felt like a bit of a rant. To get back to whatever was going on: I was having one of my vacuum attacks because I wanted the MWM to take care of me, in the knowledge that he would never do it (which is precisely what made me think he might be worthy of the post). How utterly cretinous of me. At the time, of course, I didn't really think it through, I just started walking to where I thought he'd be and (are we on miracle three or four now?) there he was. He seemed rather unsurprised at my reappearance and we continued our outing where we had left off.

Something made me ask a question that seemed to upset him and I started to feel a little better. Not simply because I'm a sadist, but more because it was an effect we'd created between us and wasn't just him talking as if he was playing with a doll or performing for a video camera with no one behind it. It was a stupid thing about whether or not he liked to imagine he was attractive to women, and which he found unnecessarily cruel. I only asked because he had just included in his monologue the observation that people fancied him more when he was having a bad time. It annoyed me because it was so untrue of me. I was finding his unease and consequent self-centredness a big drag. It pissed me off to think he might believe it was a turn-on.

We found a sunny place to sit and, despite the fact that I was deeply unsure of how I felt about him, I stroked him gently and kissed him on his face and neck. I found myself telling him that the more incapable he was of caring about me the more likely I'd be to care about him. I can't imagine why I said it. What a stupid sentiment. He was half-asleep when it came out (perhaps because I was doing the talking) so with luck he didn't hear me. But I do sometimes wonder whether he did and whether any of his actions are guided by it.

We stood up and set off once more on our ceaseless mission. By now I was feeling undeniably miserable and dejected and told him so. From being too talkative (in the worst possible way) he

137

became too silent (in the worst possible way). I told him I was going to sit on a chair and fall asleep and that he could carry on taking his photographs and I'd wake up when he finished. This turned out to be a very good move. I sat in a heap with my coat thrown over my lap like a granny and dropped off. I woke up intermittently to feel my anxieties switching themselves off one at a time like lights in a building at night. After twenty minutes I had recovered my natural ebullience enough to face the ∧∧∧. I whacked him with my wallet for being the only person I knew who could completely tire me out. We went for a drink and teased each other about what bad company we were, and when twenty-four hours were up I got on the tube to go home. No evaporations. No fantasies of self-mutilation. It was easy. I got home, climbed into bed, pronounced the ∧∧∧ to be thoroughly vile and resolved not to have lustful or romantic thoughts about him ever again.

By this time, my boyfriend had returned and asked what had happened last night. I told him I had been fast asleep and hadn't heard the bell. He gave me a disbelieving look but, typically, didn't push the point. A few days later he told the story to one of our friends adding, as a small detail, that he had heard a moan.

⌒

On the subject of terrible things I have done, I did another pretty dodgy one last night. I didn't mean to, but I guess that's no excuse. I finished work slightly later than usual as the night porter was late to come and take my place at the switchboard. It must have been about twenty past five when he finally appeared. Just as I was getting ready to go Philip walked past and said goodbye. I pulled my coat and gloves on as fast as I could and was about to run after him and try to accompany him to the station. But when I saw him walking down the street by himself I felt much more interested in finding out what he would do if I didn't interrupt him. I didn't really mean to follow him – I was actually going the same way anyhow – I was just innocently enjoying observing him. It's like when you see your cat in the garden defending its patch or chasing a bird. You realize that the dozy ball that flops around the house becomes a completely different creature on the other side of the catflap. When I saw Philip striding down towards Piccadilly Circus I wanted to watch how he would behave in the wilds of central London. Would he bump into people? Would he look in shop windows? Would he buy the *Evening Standard*? Or the *Big Issue*? I decided that when we got to the station I would either let him go or, if he was catching the same train, announce myself. But meanwhile it was more fun to just let him be.

The problem came when we came to the station entrance. Instead of going down the steps he bypassed the station and crossed over to the other side of Piccadilly Circus. It was a nice dry night and the Christmas lights were up already. I decided it wouldn't do any harm to walk with Philip a little further. He walked under the old archway and up into Golden Square. He looked at his watch and then walked round the square a couple of times. This bit was good because it was more like the sort of nerdy thing a person like Philip is meant to do and made me feel like the risk and effort of following him was paying off. After that he walked up into Beak Street, turning left. I hung around on the corner, trying to look like I was waiting for somebody. I looked at my wrist a couple of times, even though I don't have a watch. Philip turned right into another little archway. I jogged after him for fear of letting him out of my sight. When I got to the archway he was gone.

Just before I got there I heard what must have been the big black door on my right slam shut. I looked everywhere for a sign or a nameplate but couldn't see one. There was just a doorbell with no writing on it. My heart was beating really fast – I couldn't believe that Philip had done something as interesting as disappearing behind a black door in Soho. What was he up to? It could have been a friend's house for all I knew but I wanted to believe it was something more exotic.

I waited in the café over the road until six o'clock when it closed. Philip still hadn't reappeared so I decided to go home. What was he up to? What was *I* up to? I feel really awful about it now. Philip was probably doing something completely innocuous – and even if he wasn't it's none of my business – but now I have all these unfounded suspicions about him which I can't get out of my head. I wish I hadn't followed him. I'd really rather not think about it at all.

20

The End

Oh wow! I'm going to have to tell you the end of the book right now – well, not the end exactly, more like a sort of provisional end which I'd like to use as long as nothing goes too wrong in between. It will finish with me being all happy and over-excited about the /\/\/\/\ after spending a perfect weekend with him – this weekend just past. Well, maybe perfect is a bit strong, but it was definitely a marked improvement on the usual. All I'll have to do is fill in the final few bits explaining how I managed to get from hate to love and that will be that.

He still seems rather bonkers but I guess I am getting more used to it. *He* actually invited *me* to spend the weekend with him, which was unexpected and made me feel much better. I went to stay at his warehouse. Some of the other people there don't seem overly fond of him. I think they find him a little overwhelming and out-of-control. But, judging by the number of meetings they have, control is perhaps something they are a little too interested in. He found a huge green pipe in a skip which he installed, floor to ceiling, right in the middle of one of the shared rooms. His idea of a good time is to go and watch a really big crane in action. He's definitely a strange person to spend time around, but I do basically like him. A lot, in fact. I think. It's possible, if not inevitable, that it will all blow apart in the near or far future, so I've decided to quit while I'm ahead. Three cheers for the arbitrariness of happy endings.

*　　*　　*

☎☎☎ For the first time ever, I'm actually liking the phone calls more than doing this. I can just be chirpy and dumb, which is exactly how I feel. I think it's because these cheerful feelings and thoughts have grabbed me unawares and I'm reluctant to ask too many questions about them – partly because it will ruin the ending ☎ when it really comes ☎ and partly because I do have some sense of privacy and I'd like to keep all this to myself for a while. I'm also scared that if I scrutinize my feelings too closely at a moment when I'm enjoying them so much I might find out that they're quite fragile and illusory, or that they sound pitiably stupid on paper. So today we have a definite victory for life over literature. It won't last, though. Another reason for holding back on the ending is that I promised to quit the job before quitting writing. While I may momentarily be enjoying the mindlessness of it all, I could hardly be pleased about finishing on the suggestion that luck in love turns you into a blithering idiot. I haven't sorted out the boyfriend stuff yet either for that matter. I'd better not get too excited about everything as I am almost certainly on the verge of losing my home, half my friends and a person with whom I have really enjoyed spending the last four years of my life. My boyfriend wasn't exactly thrilled about my weekend disappearance – although he hasn't explicitly told me so. He was just crushingly monosyllabic on my return. It scared me a little. If we went our separate ways I would probably miss him like crazy.

Never mind. Happiness is giving me pinging sensations throughout my entire body. What a funny feeling it is.

21

Tuesday

After the twenty-four hour torment session the ∧∧∧ and I had to meet again so he could return my camera. I was rather dreading it and couldn't imagine how it would go. I was certain that after this I'd never, ever see him again, but when he rang the following Monday to organize an assignation he sounded much more like the person I'd fallen for than the person I'd suffered the previous Friday night (*and* Saturday daytime). It was funny how, having given up on him entirely, ☎ this electronically transmitted glimpse of his former self was enough to tempt me to reverse my decision completely. Whatever it was I'd seen and not liked didn't entirely exclude or eclipse the thing I was initially drawn to. They seemed as distinct as if they had been located in two different bodies. (And that's still how it feels. When all's well with the ∧∧∧ this other thing that happens with him seems nearly impossible – often you can think you've seen it for the last time. But invariably you haven't.)

Anyhow, this was one of those happy occasions where the nasty twin was locked up at home and the winsome brother was allowed an outing. We were both ten minutes early. We kissed and hugged affectionately and wandered off hand in hand to a bar with big sofas.

I told him straight away that I'd decided he was horrible and he laughed. He pointed out that the observer tends to affect the thing observed. Under the circumstances this rather threw me. I didn't want to think it was me that made the twenty-four hours go the way they did. Did my being around him turn him into what he was? I thought *he* was making *me* behave oddly. Then maybe my slight oddness (I was hardly in my normal frame of mind) exacerbated his oddness, which in turn made mine even worse, which he found hard to deal with so he responded even more oddly to the point where I finally passed out. This unmanageable horribleness that we'd made together was like a complex chemical reaction. It wasn't entirely caused by either of us, or made from the same substance as either of us, but something in the combination of both of us brought it about. This Tuesday, maybe because we knew how things could go if we weren't careful, it didn't happen. No strange concoctions of interpersonal effect – just a very pleasant evening. I don't remember much of what we talked about, I just remember lolling comfortably on a couch having a thoroughly nice time. The only two bits of speech I recall were his mention of the fact that it was his twenty-ninth birthday the following Friday which, stupidly, made me think it might be a nice day to see him, and his passionate disapproval of my dress. It seemed so nondescript to me – it was just a knee-length black thing with a small picture of some butterflies coming out of an envelope on the front. When I asked why he found it so awful he told me, 'My dear, as everybody knows, butterflies come from *larves*.'

Afterwards, he walked me to the tube station and we parted quite amicably (although he did say that he was going to watch me go through the barriers and see them slam behind me to make sure I didn't reappear). He asked if he could hang on to my camera, though, so I decided not to get too offended. I was glad to have at least one thing he needed. I guess I imagined that the more he continued to borrow the camera, the more he would be forced to notice all the other things I had that he needed too. While I see that this may sound a bit doormattish, it also shows what a strong belief I have in my own seductive powers. I felt sure that if he knew me better he'd realize how great I was. It's a strange, yet very common way of understanding oneself – at the same time as being the most terrible person you are also the most wonderful. I guess the main point is that, in both cases, you are 'the most' and this 'mostness' is the bit you're after.

He's a funny person. A cameraless photographer. Isn't this like being a dumb singer? I suppose it shows that he takes pictures because he really wants to, rather than because he just happens to have the equipment lying around. I find it a mixture of admirable and pathetic. If I wasn't so pleased about his cameralessness for romantic reasons I think I would insist on him buying his own. He is very far from rich, though, and I understand that this is a serious drawback.

∽

Just now it occurred to me how much I'd like to have his side of the story. I imagine it would be fantastically different to this one. It's strange, but when all this sort of stuff is going on it tends to flatten the other person out for you. You can start to imagine that you're the only one having thoughts and feelings – that the other person forgets who you are as soon as you say goodbye and wanders off into a placid universe of peaceful activity and restful sleep (or worse, unimaginable pleasures).

I'd ask people what they thought might be going on – why he was so slack about calling and so cool about lovey things – and was invariably told that men don't have too many wistful thoughts about women when they're not around or that, if they ever do, they're simply thoughts about shagging or women in general. The idea that a man could muster a romantic feeling is popularly presumed to be out of the question. It seems that plenty of otherwise reasonable people actually believe this. ♥

22

Cash

Now I'm really, really sick of being a receptionist and would like to stop. I still don't know what I expect from life, but this has just become untenable. I need to get away. I had hoped I would leave before the office party, but it's happening tomorrow, so I'll either have to be sick, or grin and bear it. I have never been to an office party in my life and I find the idea horrifying. Maybe I've received a warped idea of office parties from newspaper and magazine articles on the subject, but I don't want to see these people when they're drunk. I am afraid that it is only in their inhibited form I am able to tolerate them.

〜

The office manager has just yelled at me again. She was dressed in a kind of nylon mint blancmange and shook like a pudding as she emphasized important points with her finger. What set her off was this dumb package I told you about before. I have no idea who bloody Sir Lippoch is, so how can I give him his parcel? I asked all the secretaries whether they recognized the name and they each said no. I asked the people in the postroom if they could help me trace the owner but they told me it was my problem if I signed for packages without reading the name first. I etched the letters onto my brain in case one of the old men ever matched it or mentioned it. I even tried directory inquiries. I decided the best thing to do would be to hang on to it in case the same courier came back and I could return it to its sender. But this apparently isn't good enough for the office manager. She ordered two hundred rounds of sandwiches for a four-person conference in the boardroom today and needs to prove that other people are fallible too. She told me that two days was the longest I should ever allow a package to remain in reception before tracing its owner or sending it back. This package has been here for weeks. She told me that I'd better sort it out *fast* and that she would check in a few days to see what I had done about it. I have decided that the best solution is to stick it under the table and hope she forgets. I don't imagine she is efficient enough to follow up her threat.

Heck has just been up to change the light bulbs. The Academy has four great big, multi-fronded chandeliers in the front hall and the bulbs are always blowing. Maintaining these is probably the most aggravating and strenuous part of Heck's job. Each time a bulb blows Heck has to drag the ladder upstairs, drag his body up the ladder, drag his arms up to reach the bulb, sort it out, and then drag the whole lot downstairs again. In Werner Herzog's *Fitzcaraldo* some of the actors died dragging a heavy boat over the top of a mountain. Heck acts like one of these actors. However, for some reason, today his evil temper is offset by a minute trace of cheerfulness. I ask him if he is looking forward to the office party. He sneers at me and then follows his sneer with a weird laugh and shakes his head. I wonder what this laugh means. He tells me he won't be here tomorrow, or ever again. I ask him what he's going to do instead and he just shrugs. I hope he isn't planning on freezing to death in a playground or something. I wonder whether he decided to leave, or was sacked. Either way, it's impressive news. This definitely seemed like the wrong place for Heck, but I can't picture any place that would be right – apart from a big couch tended by devoted servants. I hope he's going to be all-right. Heck's departure should give me courage, but instead it fills me with dread. What will happen to him when he leaves the Academy? What would happen to me if I left the Academy? How could the Academy be so irresponsible as to let him go without checking whether or not he'll be okay?

~

What shall I do? I can't sit around for whole days at a time doing nothing (except this). I need to be out doing stuff, but I don't know quite what stuff to do. There are so few things you can get money for that I don't hate doing. The only thing I think I'd like is to get paid to act like I normally do and be followed by an invisible observer for research purposes. Then all the unbelievably minor things I enjoy (window shopping, meeting friends, looking at things, sitting in parks, talking to strangers) would become legitimate working activities. I may start doing the lottery again too. Oh no, actually. That's a terrible idea. The best idea would be to make this book really good and get a big advance. I heard of someone my age the other day who got a £30,000 advance for her first novel. But it was a thriller, not this sort of low-budget, not-much-happening type of book. £30,000! I get £164 a week for thirty-five hours of torture. That's 7.8 pence a minute. It would take me three hundred and eighty-four thousand six hundred and fifteen point three minutes to earn £30,000 as a receptionist. And you should experience how long a minute can take in this place. A minute as a receptionist equals at least two minutes spent waiting for a bus in the rain, three minutes reading a Jeffrey Archer novel, four minutes hoovering or five minutes watching daytime television. Would anyone agree to watch thirty-two thousand and fifty-one point three hours of Richard and Judy in return for a poxy thirty grand? I would rather take part in a dangerous, long-term cryogenic experiment for nothing.

Anyhow, it would take me three-and-a-half years' worth of endless receptionist's minutes to earn what this girl got for writing a thriller. Shit.

23

Master/Slave *Dial*ectics

The Academy has its Christmas office party at lunchtime, after which everyone is supposed to go back to work. I imagine it's going to be a pretty restrained affair (no time for slobbering or falling over or shagging on top of the photocopiers). A boy has been hired to replace me while we eat. No one else needs to be replaced so I guess, in one respect, I am the most important person in the office. Maybe they will put me at the head of the table. Apparently it doesn't work like this, though. No one is placed above anyone – today is the one day of the year when the office hierarchy is relaxed. When we enter the dining room, we will draw a number from a hat to find out where we will be sitting.

After making such a fuss about the whole status and eating thing I really ought to be happy, but I'm not. I'm dreading it. I would hate to sit next to the director. I can hardly understand him when he speaks and would be afraid of his spit showers landing on my food. I would also hate to get stuck next to the slow-speaking wood-lady. After a couple of glasses of wine I think I would find it very hard to stay awake. The finance man could be hard work too. His conversational clumsiness makes me very uneasy, but perhaps we could help each other out with some career advice. I'd love to end up next to Philip. The would-be-fireman said he had a way of rigging the seating, but that I'd have to be sick to want to sit with 'that useless freak'. He said I could sit at his table, with all the other young people at the Academy. It seems a bit like copping out, but I think I

149

might take him up on his offer. I would be really annoyed if I turned him down and then found myself next to the office manager.

I ought to take today seriously, though, as it is one of the few occasions I get, as a receptionist, to bring about world change. If I have lunch with the directors and talk to them, perhaps they will feel differently about their positions in relation to mine, and all the other people whom they previously understood as being 'below' them. Perhaps they will talk about this startling change amongst themselves and their director friends. Perhaps other directors will begin to have lunch with their receptionists and postmen and cleaners, and discover that they like it. Perhaps they will start to feel funny about getting paid so much more than all their new companions, and do something to rectify the situation. If I can only handle the office party right, the world might become a better place.

I'm not sure I am charismatic enough to bring about this sort of reform, but that's no excuse for not trying. I really don't want to sit next to that spluttering old codger, though. What a dilemma.

The time has come. My replacement is here. I am off to the library for a pre-lunch drink.

～

I didn't do it. The would-be-fireman somehow got hold of all the tickets for one of the tables and handed them out to people he liked. I probably should have refused, but I didn't want to seem ungracious. I sat between him and a man I hadn't really noticed before who has a hole in his forehead big enough to stick your fingertip in. Also on our table were the personnel woman, the pretty girl in accounts and a miserable boy who said he didn't like parties. We all obediently read out the jokes on our crackers and tried not to talk about office things. The

150

would-be-fireman told everyone that the mark on my face was from a piercing and that he had seen me sticking it back in after work. They all found this disgusting and incomprehensible. No one asked the man with the hole in his head where he got his from. Maybe they already know. He has a long moustache and shoulder-length white hair and looks like a sheriff in a Western. I suspect he got the hole playing war simulation games at weekends. Maybe it's something more serious. It's a good hole anyway, but for some reason it seems to be taboo to discuss it.

Like at the Royal outcasts' lunch, everyone said how much they preferred our table to all the other tables as there was no authority figure around to restrain us. Like last time, this was a load of bollocks. It was really boring. I wished the ex-receptionist was still here.

I kept looking over at Philip to see how he was getting on. He didn't exactly seem like the life and soul of the party. He was looking down into his plate most of the time and not speaking to anyone. I wished I had insisted on sitting next to him. Since I followed him that day I have felt so guilty I have been avoiding him. It would have been nice to have had a glass of wine with him and a jovial Christmas chat. I wonder what he'll be doing over the break. One of the secretaries in his department told me that his mother was very ill and he was very worried about her. I hope he won't be spending it alone.

After the meal there was a raffle with about twenty prizes (of varying degrees of crapness) none of which I won. And then we all went back to work. I wonder what it was like for the people at the other tables. Maybe they have managed to alter something somehow. I feel quite perplexed by the whole non-event. I was only half joking about this world-changing thing. But the office party has made me think differently. I don't think the world is up to the job of being any other way.

Why do people like to imagine that it is the Director or Department Manager who keeps them in check when it is perfectly obvious that they are held back by themselves. These people all seem to come with built-in bosses, which is why it's so easy for their external bosses to boss them around – it's a simple case of two against one.

Most of us (including our bosses) need bosses in order to stay sane. Even the people who are ostensibly at the very top of the whole heap (like the Queen or the Prime Minister) have to behave like servants in order for the social machine to function properly. If they don't see themselves as servile, and start doing funny stuff just because they feel like it, the whole system gets fucked and they have to be kicked out and replaced by a meeker version.

We cling on to hierarchies because they make us feel safe – without our bosses we fear the whole world might degenerate into irreparable chaos. We are probably right. Life would be horrible without other people to keep us in order and tell us what to do. To compensate for this very sad fact, we make the necessity of our eternal servitude bearable by continually protesting against it.

Office parties are here to teach us that the office is like it normally is with good reason. Without our bosses in their boss role, we must either turn to our built-in bosses – whose existence we hate to acknowledge – or risk turning into unruly beasts. (This latter was what the tabloids led me to believe the Christmas party would be like – I can't decide whether I am pleased or disappointed.) External bosses are essential to our capacity to see ourselves as nice (mistreated) people.

〜

I think I may have been at the Academy a little too long. What would the ex-receptionist have to say about all this? I need guidance. I think he would probably just tell me I was a sad twat who could hope for nothing better than to drown in a puddle and putrefy. Perhaps this is what I need to hear to snap me out of my miserable wrongness. Although I fear I may actually have a point.

(Look! I am cultivating a built-in ex-receptionist to counterbalance my built-in boss. This is very encouraging, but I'm concerned that, if he takes over, he may not be capable of controlling my dormant psychopath.)

24

Behind the Scenes

Last week I found out about a couple of the complicated things that were affecting my love-life without my knowledge. I had a few days away from the Academy over Christmas and it gave me time to work some things out. I went to Norfolk to see my Mum and Dad and spent a couple of hours every day tramping around in the mud, cogitating. One of the main things I decided to work out once and for all was which boyfriend I was better off sticking with. I weighed up the advantages of each one: a beautiful flat, stability and a good friendship on the one side, and sex, drama and infatuation on the other. I weighed up the disadvantages: literary competition, stability and no sex versus lunacy, communes and desperate lack of keenness. I compared Christmas presents: a sparkly pink lip jewel and copy of *Tristram Shandy* from the boyfriend and absolutely fuck all from the ∧∧∧∧. I considered the option of having two boyfriends, which I know works well for some people. I decided it wouldn't for me. I would hate to share either of them with another person so I don't think I could enjoy doing it the other way round. I think I also prefer the focus necessary for a monogamous relationship. I don't know. The only conclusion I came to was one I borrowed from someone else. A student of Freud's once went to him to ask advice about something that was bothering him – he had a big decision to make and didn't know how best to approach it. Freud advised him that when making small, pragmatic decisions it was best to weigh up all the pros and cons and try as best you could to come to a considered conclusion. But when you had to make up your mind about something big – like marriage or babies or dramatic changes of lifestyle – it was best to just trust your impulses and do what you felt like. This has always struck me as very good advice. The problem in this instance is that I would love to be able to follow it but fear I may be prevented from doing so by the nature of the decision I have to make. The /\/\/\/\ is certainly the person I would choose in terms of where my impulse leads me. But what if I decide in his favour and then find out that he doesn't want to know me? I will lose my home and a boyfriend for whom I genuinely feel a lot of things. But what if I decide in favour of my boyfriend because I am afraid of losing a situation which I can tolerate, but don't exactly enjoy? I could end up being sad and bored for the rest of my life. I've gone over this dilemma so many times now I don't know what to say. Ultimately, the best strategy I can think up is that I should do what I feel like in so far as I can and then cobble together the best possible result from the outcome.

What happened to that promise of a happy ending?

As I've said, my main problem with the /\/\/\/\ has been that his character seems to me very opaque and indecipherable. Well, a small part of this inscrutability might have been coming from certain misunderstandings that were completely beyond my control (and certain ones that weren't – like the boyfriend). One thing was that one of my very best friends – a cigarette-thin, wig-wearing hysteric from Barcelona – got it into his head to threaten the /\/\/\/\ with violence. I only found out because, the night before I went away, my friend confessed rather sheepishly to what he'd done. It slipped out over the course of a three-hour telephone conversation about his love-life, during which he alternately sobbed, ranted, swigged more gin and got mad and maudlin like someone in a Rossellini film.

I called the /\/\/\/\ on Christmas day to wish him well and, while I was at it, tried to bring the threat scene up with him. But he rather shirked the issue. Why didn't he want to talk about it? And why did it happen anyway?

This is the sort of event that I have little hope of ever comprehending. I'd told the friend about my crush as soon as it started. He was actually the one who introduced us at that art opening in the summer so I thought he ought to know. He went berserk asking why I couldn't develop the good taste to fancy smaller, neater people. Finally he gave up all hope of converting me. Instead he decided to take up my cause against the MMM's careless and inattentive ways. On the way back from a party – accompanied by the small troll who was causing him so much heartache at the time – my friend ran into the MMM at a bus stop. He launched immediately into his favourite speech (it's not the first time he's done it). He stands with his hands on his hips and tells the person listening that they'd better be nice to [whoever] because [whoever] is his very best friend. He warns that if he hears about any misbehaviour there'll be very big trouble. Finally he looks the person straight in the eye and says, 'So watch out or you'll have *me* to answer to'. It must come as a surprise if you're not expecting it. I'm sure it was quite offputting. What could the MMM have imagined it meant? He might have thought I must either be very, very nice or very, very fragile if my friends were so keen to look after me. Or he may have thought my friend was insane (and perhaps me by association). Did it really happen even? Maybe he thought I came from a very religious family and that my chastity was important enough to become a public issue. But obviously all this is ridiculous and implausible. It's possible I'm being a bit dense, but I can't think of any explanation that would do. The whole thing seems to expose a big gash in my framework for understanding the world. Is that dumb of me? It's such a trifling thing and I'm sure people do that stuff to each other all the time, but for some reason my brain can't process it. What made my friend decided to do that to me? Does he just contain a mechanical impulse that causes him to make his speech at regular intervals, or does he have to have a reason? Why can't I understand people? Why, at certain moments, do I find that even those closest to me become as mystifying as the most strange and elusive deep-sea fish?

∽

A short while later I stumbled across some sort of answer to this question. The reason I couldn't make sense of the situation is to be found in my wilful capacity to misread. How comforting it would have been to believe that the MM actually listened to this threat and was prevented from showing more enthusiasm due to it, rather than due to the fact that he didn't find me attractive, that he was involved with someone else, that he had more important things on his mind, that he had hardly registered my existence at all. How nice to 'know' the reason for his lack of eagerness, and for it to have no damning reflection on me. Frankly, I would have *loved* this threat to have been the cause of his not-phoning (and it's dramatic and romantic too). But something didn't match up. It didn't quite do the job I wanted it to. I didn't want to confront the reasons why he'd failed to contact me, so I conjured up a new set of enigmatic reasons and hoped they'd shield me from the possibilities I wanted to avoid.

The funny thing is, though, that some of these unthinkably horrible reasons were actually true, but nonetheless, as you already know, the story has a happy ending. Perhaps it's lucky I didn't acknowledge them, or I might not have persevered. My most revolting discovery was that the MM was sleeping with someone else when I met him. I wheedled it out of him after I got back from Norfolk. I went round to his commune and found a fax sent on Christmas day with a row of kisses at the bottom. This surplus girl is entirely extraneous to *my* story, though (and I would hate to honour her with a leading role in

157

my novel) so, if you feel the need to know about this sordid little episode, you can read about it in the unnumbered and altogether unnecessary chapter that follows this one.

‿

It was shortly after the nice Tuesday meeting in the bar with sofas that the friend confessed his sins to me and I squeaked with confusion and told him that above all he must mend his ways and put an end to his mischief. This is the wrong thing to say to a friend like this as he takes it to heart and tries to patch things up. He bumped into the ⋀⋀⋀ on his birthday – which he had chosen to celebrate without me – and did an equally devastating performance. This time he decided to tell him repeatedly to ring me. The effect on the ⋀⋀⋀ was indeed that he rang the very next day, but not sounding particularly cheery.

We met in the park and I was rather late – which put him in a foul temper. He was looking unusually boyish in a denim jacket, jeans and sporty top. We ambled about chatting quite confessionally, and this is when he told me that he didn't like other people knowing his business and interfering with it and would rather I didn't chatter too much to my friends about our thing and would appreciate a little less hassle from this particular friend who had really wound him up to the point where he had almost vowed to himself that he would never ring me again (which, in mathematical terms, wouldn't be a huge reduction in phonecalls). Despite the shaky start, the more we chatted the better things got and after a couple of hours things got very good indeed and we kissed a lot and did something quite naughty, which I'm afraid I'm not going to tell you about. (I'm tired of those little ☎ signs, so I'll just tell you in words that the phones are going nuts at work. I'm becoming super-double-misanthropic and have lost my capacity to be polite to people.) Then we ate and had the sort of evening that people

158

who aren't psychotic and who actually like each other have. It was quite a relief. It made a nice change to act like an average boyfriend and girlfriend instead of a pair of paranoid saddos. It left me feeling very happy, but also a little anxious about the consequences of this sort of comforting happiness. Would one or two more meetings like this transform the ∿∿∿ and me into an ordinary couple? (I ought to admit that I only have a very hazy idea of what I might mean by this and I'm not at all sure I'm convinced by the notion in general). I know plenty of couples and have been part of quite a few and the idea wasn't immediately appealing. It's one of those irreducible problems: you get infatuated and all you want is more and more of the person and then you get it and you feel a bit stuck and don't know what to do with it. I guess this is a bad sign in favour of boyfriend-changing being an escapist and arbitrary enterprise. But that sounds a bit too dismal in relation to how I feel right now. I think I'm still hoping to meet the person of my dreams and fall in love for ever and ever. And a rather dumb part of me is hoping this person will turn out to be the ∿∿∿.

⌐

I feel so bad today about writing true stories. I feel guilty on two counts. Firstly I feel bad because, at least amongst my immediate circle of friends, everyone knows who's who and some of them might be embarrassed. And secondly because these sorts of stories are quite difficult to follow because they make so little sense. Made-up stories tend to follow some kind of production logic that means the parts all relate to each other in ways constructed by the story's narrative dynamic. But these real stories are more like games of consequences: you can only see a fraction of the other person's stuff so your response is guided by a partial knowlege of what's going on, producing an end result of a fractured whole whose parts are an odd mix of sense and nonsense. Perhaps that's one of the keys to the

159

difference between made-up stories and true ones – that with fiction it's been processed through a single organism who has done their best to round it into some sort of completion (even with open-ended stories, whose open-endedness constitutes an integral part of their sense). This story too is being processed through a single organism (me), but it's partly being dictated by other people (the ∧∧∧, my parents, my boyfriend, the impossible friend, the office) and it's all I can do to record it, let alone throw light on it, decipher it and deliver it to you in compact and comprehensible form. So much for writing about what you know. As soon as you start you realize that you don't even know it any more.

〜

By some freak coincidence I have just been told over the phone by the ∧∧∧ that my meddlesome friend has been meddling *again*, but he refused to tell me then and there what the content of this meddling was. He rather kindly hinted that it wasn't altogether terrible, but this is giving me little comfort.

(Optional)

The Flea

During the crying incident which marked the beginning of my terrible infatuation there was a droopy-looking girl lurking in the background. I decided she must be a flatmate or dismal hanger-on. But this dull girl was actually having an affair with the /\/\/\/\. Few things could have been more repulsive to me than this piece of information. I know I'm with him now – and that he couldn't possibly have predicted my rudely bursting in and interrupting his life at that precise moment – but this particular bit of his history disturbs me. Why was it so difficult for *me* to get his attention when he was prepared to give it to that dishrag of a person? I know it's good that he didn't just drop her and shows he can be nice, but it still pisses me off. I told *him* I had a boyfriend – why didn't he mention her? Maybe he was hedging his bets. Or maybe he was embarrassed. She was a pointless thing in jeans. A TV-catchphrase-repeating, cuddly-toy-owner of a girl.

Taking all the evidence into account, this is how I have chosen to interpret it: The flea was one of those sorry beings who wanted to administrate art for a living. Perhaps it was the only way she believed she could meet 'interesting' people. She was kind to any artists she came across, telling them their work was either 'damn good' or 'funky' and offering to help them lug it about. While they were hanging it she would stand back with her finger on her chin, cock her head to one side and squint. The artists (namely the /\/\/\/\) would appreciate this service and think that she was doing it specially for them – instead of it being a bit of career practice. They might even get so grateful they'd want to sleep with her.

One might imagine that this was what she wanted, but it doesn't seem to have been so simple. She would do the sex thing until the work experience was over and then find a reason to abandon the artist, using her career as an excuse: either she couldn't be with him because her aspirations kept her in a particular place, or she'd leave him to chase a job somewhere else. She dumped the ∧∧∧– rather unceremoniously – a few days after our first night together (which he didn't tell her about) to go for a job in America. She wanted him to carry on liking her after her departure though – for purely vain reasons – so she kept in touch and pretended she'd try to get a show for him once she got there.

∽

What a crappy way to go about life – you choose a job that will enable you to meet 'interesting people', and then allow this job to become more important than the 'interesting people' you meet through it. How symptomatic of having no idea what you want. You are unsure of what will make you happy, so you get a job looking after people whom you believe are doing what they really love. You hope that being near these people will fill up the hole left by your own lack of directed desire. You find out that it doesn't go like that and that being near these people is neither more fulfilling, nor less difficult, than being near anyone else. You swap your expectations of what they will bring for your expectations of what the job will bring – money, respect (from other people who still believe that working with artists is different to working with other categories of human being), a bit of travel – and continue to fritter away your short life. Perhaps you even become cynical about humanity as you become increasingly reliant on comfort to compensate for the more rarified rewards you imagined your association with 'interesting people' would bring.

The MWM still writes to this girl – via his friend's e-mail – and it makes me mad. She suggests she may put his work in an exhibition alongside Marcel Duchamp's, and he gets all excited and replies to her at once. (She is now working as a very junior curator and has no power whatsoever to actualize this plan.) Having ascertained that he is still somehow in her clutches, she seems to feel a little better and lets him know that this show isn't actually going to happen, but that she'll keep him posted and nominate him for shows in the future (with Andy Warhol, or Damian Hirst, or whatever other big art name she can remember at that moment.)

The MWM has finally told this creature about me (although he took his time about it). I think she is a little worried about who I might be and has begun playing a rather crude game of *fort da* with him, hoping to renegotiate a position in his life. It appears she can only enjoy getting rid of people if she can pull the strings to get them back.

This is the risk of not taking risks: if you aren't prepared to do the difficult things you may have to do in order to get what you want, you are very likely to end up with nothing. (Maybe nothing *is* what she wants, in which case I wish she'd stop using the MWM on her circuitous mission to get it.)

How does being a receptionist compare with being a curator? Surely taking other people's telephone calls is the archetypal vicarious job. Why am I tearing into this poor woman, who is probably just a nice person doing her best?

I'll tell you. Firstly, I am not a receptionist. And secondly, even if I was, receptionists don't do what they do because they think it will make them more like the people they do it for. They do it precisely because they don't want to be like the people who work upstairs in their office. They would hate to take job worries home with them, or to compete with their 'friends' for promotions, or to have to stay late in order to get things done. Most receptionists are too smart to want to have 'proper' jobs. They are too busy with their own stuff – having difficult love-lives, telephoning their friends, reading, writing, making complex calculations – to want to bother with actual work. Receptionists feel only pity for their colleagues.

Curators, on the other hand, seem to believe that mere proximity is glory and are thus always cheating themselves out of having any fun. They worry, compete and stay late – and then find out that the artists they were hoping to share the limelight with are off having a much better time with receptionists.

(Shit. I'm getting really receptionisty. Receptionists are always saying rubbish like this. We're a really defensive bunch. We get so worried about people thinking we're worse than them that we go around inventing reasons why we're better. We're always hung-up about being seen as stupid. Ask any receptionist what she's reading and she'll tell you Dostoyevsky. We're not entirely wrong to worry, though. People find it perfectly acceptable to sneer about the inferiority of receptionists in ways that would be quite forbidden concerning any other social group. Look at the Philadelphia cheese advertisements and the countless 'thick telephonist' comedy sketches. They always portray us as having fey, sing-song voices, pink lips and fluffy hair. Check out the nail-painting moron at the entrance to the brain surgeon's office in *Total Recall*. Ask your friends to describe a typical receptionist and you'll see what effect these representations have on popular consciousness. Even at the beginning of *The Mezzanine*, Nicholson Baker writes the most outrageous bit of nonsense about the tastelessness of receptionists' perfumes. Receptionists are one of the few remaining sections of society it's thought perfectly okay to be rude about.)

What is the ᴹᴹᴹ's investment in this setup? He seems to me truly extraordinary and not someone who needs to laze around imagining being next to famous artists in place of actually doing his work. His work's really good and he does loads of it. He definitely doesn't seem to be an artist because of some trashy fantasy about artists being superior, but because he actually finds making things interesting. I'm sure he doesn't require some vapid parasite to pretend to help him get on. I have a fantasy that if I show the depth of my feeling for him – in words, in gestures and in time – he will no longer feel the need to lean on a rickety crutch like this ex-shag. I wonder whether I am being naïve.

He occasionally suggests that I might like her if I met her. How could I possibly like a girl who behaves in this way with the person I'm in love with? Perhaps I do give her a slightly bad press, but if she did anything to suggest that she had a single redeeming feature, I would certainly change my mind. I'm sorry to say that I always read the e-mails she sends him, and repeatedly find myself wishing that she would do me the courtesy of occasionally writing something interesting. She just tells him piles of inarticulate crap about all the artists she's had to speak to on the phone and how it was 'just so cool', like a dumb groupie.

That the ᴹᴹᴹ hasn't yet told her to fuck off is deeply upsetting to me. Why does he like her hanging around (albeit virtually)? Maybe he enjoys being treated like an 'artist'. Maybe he likes her because she is dull and distant, and doesn't give him any trouble.

I hope she reads this and drops dead from irritation and embarrassment.

25

Losses and Gains

I'm so jumpy today. I feel like I've lost everything. I've lost my flat (I don't care). I've lost my chequebook and card (I don't care much). I've lost my favourite lipstick and new eyeliner (I do care). And I've lost some jewellery. (Why on earth would you care about what I care about?) Philip has also been away for the last few days and, for some reason, I have started to worry about him.

To top it all I have been made January's Temp of the Month, and have lost a large portion of my self-respect.

⌐

Yes, it's true. I've just lost my home. It has finally been decided. I have a month to move out. The boyfriend and I tentatively agreed that living together was becoming a little difficult – although we didn't actually agree to give up the flat. What happened was that we started talking to our friends and family about what was going on, in the hope of being given some guiding words of wisdom – or at least a little sympathy. Word got out that we were separating. And, more importantly, that our beautiful, inexpensive flat might shortly be available. One of our caring commiserators went to the landlord, explained the problem, and put in an offer for the flat (which included an extensive refurbishment without any financial input from him). The next thing we knew we had four weeks to find new homes. Once we no longer had our apartment to hold us together it

166

became pretty clear that we didn't have much else either. We were still friends, in a sort of hurt and complicated way, but we certainly weren't going to move into a new place together.

Whatever you might think about the action of our landlord-courting friend, I believe he did us a giant favour. I couldn't imagine what this would mean before it happened but now it's become a reality I'll just have to deal with it. The whole thing is actually a big relief. The boyfriend has also been running around after a married woman he met at a party – which makes me feel much less guilty. I don't even feel sad. I wonder what made us hang in there for so long. Sometimes these desperately postponed disasters are really nothing when they actually take place. There was no big splitting-up scene, or even a moment you could point at to say when it actually happened. He and I seem to be parting on fairly good terms – but as we've never gone in for fighting, I suppose we would be unlikely to start now. I think the moral of this story is that, if you don't start as you mean to go on, and keep going on in the manner of this bad start, you'll finish up in the way that you started wondering what on earth happened in between. The unobtrusiveness of the ending is perhaps the saddest thing about the whole story, but I definitely don't feel like crying. I'm just really looking forward to seeing what will happen next.

&

I think I remember, before all this other stuff got in the way, that I was right in the middle of trying to find out what my annoying friend had said this time. His third and newest interference was that he told the ∕∖∕∖∕∖ that I liked him very much and told him to be nice to me because I'm very special (ahhh!).[1]

---

[1] I just had to tell you, because it seems to me so extraordinary, that after a morning of misery, resentment and intense boredom, the switchboard just rang and answering it gave me a feeling of extreme erotic pleasure.

This really is the last thing I would have wanted anyone to say to the MMM. I felt furiously ashamed and scolded my poor friend, who felt horrible. The friend did suggest though that, as it was true, the MMM might as well know it. He said it was merely my Englishness that was holding me back and that he was prepared to use his latin temperament in my service. This view was a new one on me and certainly not something I'd considered. What I had considered was that the MMM didn't seem to like me nearly as much as I wanted him to and that any sign of real affection from me would either utterly repel him and make him disappear, or would make him hang about and treat me like a sorry idiot. I imagined this so strongly and absolutely that nothing could have persuaded me otherwise. And I would have carried on acting in accordance with this belief to the detriment of my own happiness.

My friend's pronouncement had a most unexpected effect on the MMM. Suddenly he began to show quite overtly that he liked me, and his liking changed him in a way that made me like him more. Since the benign interference I had also been fortunate enough to resolve my former boyfriend troubles and was quite ready for a bit of encouragement from the MMM. He came to collect me for lunch at the Academy, all smiling and sweet. He picked me up outside the front door and carried me down the street, kissing me and spinning round in circles. Then he asked me if I'd like to spend the rest of my life with him. I doubt he meant it, but it was nice anyway. He was quite effusive, but in a much more non-bonkers, approachable way. This alteration is exactly what I would have chosen, though I'm not at all certain why it happened. It seems too trite to imagine that he just wanted to know I cared – although it appears that was a big part of it. I could start trying to invent infinite explanations, but the most important fact for me was that suddenly he was different and in a very good way.

That Saturday night in bed I had this very strange feeling that there was nothing missing and I wasn't hanging around waiting for some unattainable improvement. I told him straight away, as I felt that, if I didn't, the feeling might disappear. He seemed really pleased and it unlocked something in both of us making it much easier to speak. The most incredible coincidence was that we found ourselves talking about our childhoods and it turned out his parents had gone on holiday for three months when he was three years old. It made him so mad he set his grandmother's curtains on fire and was forced to bite soap as a punishment. It was substantial proof in favour of us being made for each other. Now I feel really close to him and properly in love like it's genuinely about him and isn't just a handful of fixed ideas about what love is.

We also spent a perfectly miserable Sunday evening together. He suffers a condition he calls Sundayitis, whereby he gets all melancholic at about seven o'clock in the evening and has to telephone his family. Knowing all these new things about him makes me like him more and feel more relaxed around him. These are precisely the kind of vital details I felt were noticably lacking before. Suddenly his loopiness seems like a different thing. Whereas before his rants, shrieks and schemes came across as slightly threatening, now that I have some idea of the feelings motivating them they can be included amongst his many captivating features. When he yells, 'This is a robbery!' in the corner shop or throws himself into hedges I can tell myself he is doing it to show off because he is crazy about *me*.

I decided it was about time I told him that my boyfriend was now an ex. He was quite relieved, but asked why I hadn't talked about the whole thing earlier. This seems to have been one of the main impediments to his attachment to me – that he thought I was having a sly affair and didn't have very serious feelings about him. I told him I didn't want to say things were over with the boyfriend until they really, really were. I hate people going on about how their relationship is dead, their partner doesn't understand them, etc., etc., in order to persuade other people that there's no moral problem about going to bed with them.

I think until people are both openly agreed that their thing is finished, there is a problem with starting something new. I was certainly hesitant about splitting up with my boyfriend and it's only really by a configuration of various accidents and other people's lack of tact and scruple that things have ended up this way.

(The side of the story I didn't tell him, but which was equally true, was that I would have felt stupid suddenly announcing that we were morally free to be with one another when I wasn't at all sure he wanted to be with me.)

All this second-guessing and tactical behaviour is so dumb, isn't it? But I think sometimes it's all you can do. If people went round being completely honest all the time, they'd drive each other mad. Imagine the beginning of a love affair where both people actually described all their feelings and intentions. It might occasionally be interesting, but most of the time it would probably prevent anything happening at all. Maybe this would be good. Maybe it would spare a lot of people a lot of misery. But maybe sparing yourself misery is a bad idea. I don't know. Maybe sometimes you're honest and sometimes you're not and it's a strange game of chance and intuition that makes you decide which one to be. I'm not sure why I handled it the way I did, but I don't know how else I could have done it. Anyhow, we like each other and, if that's the point of the game, then I guess we must have done okay.

Another very surprising thing has happened. The ⋀⋀⋀⋀ gave me permission to borrow his character for my novel. I told him all about it and he said he'd be flattered. I warned him that he wasn't exactly an angel in it, but he'd be wholly redeemed by the ending. He has already been used as inspiration for a character in a South American soap opera called *The Flight of the Ostrich* and is quite familiar with the business of being fictionalized. Let's face it, I've been pretty slack about keeping quiet about him, but now I'm actually allowed to have him in. It's a big relief as I would hate to upset him now that I like him so much. It would have been awful to have a happy ending in the book only for the book to come along and spoil it in real life.

I don't know what to call him now. His real name is Hipolito Maidana. Maybe I could give him a name like Bob or David, just for the last few pages. But it sounds silly. It really suits him to be called the MMM, perhaps because the shape evokes his hairstyle.

～

Philip has been away for three days now and I'm getting really worried. I have no evidence to support this hunch, but I feel like something's up. Maybe I am freaking out about Philip because my own life is going so well. I can't believe it's possible that there may be nothing much wrong right now. I asked the tinkly-voiced old lady whether she had heard from him and she said she hadn't. She said something about his mother still being unwell. I asked her whether she thought it was unusual that he hadn't called in sick or anything. She paused and then said 'no' quite defensively as if I was prying or trying to get him into trouble. I also asked the secretaries on his floor if they knew what was going on and they all agreed it must be something to do with his mum. When the would-be-fireman caught us discussing Philip's mother he started on the *Psycho* thing again, which the secretaries found hilarious.

I don't know why I can't just accept the idea that Philip might be looking after a sick old lady. The black door incident must have permanently impregnated my brain with the idea that he is caught up in some funny business. I hope he reappears tomorrow.

～

The worst thing that's happened to me today is that my temping agency has decided to make me Temp of the Month. What am I going to tell my friends? I can't imagine how they picked me out from all those other temps for this particular form of persecution. I suppose my plan to become a perfect receptionist actually worked.

I remember seeing the Temp of the Month wall when I went for my interview with the agency. It showed a row of photographs of gauche looking people sitting at computers, shaking hands with a glamorous blonde woman in a suit. Under each photo was the name of the winning temp. Come to think of it, it wasn't unlike the row of ex-presidents we have on the wall here – so this kind of thing *does* happen occasionally. The only difference is that, while the ex-presidents have pompous portraits, mounted and framed in gold, the temps' photographs are grotty snapshots stuck to the wall with blu-tack. I remember being quite horrified by the whole notion and imagining myself very different to the temps in the photos. I felt that they were pitiable, commited temporary workers, while I was merely someone using temping as a step towards greater things. Now I am one of them. I have been given a large bunch of flowers and some Marks and Spencer vouchers. I have also been given a certificate saying what a nice, presentable, reliable and charming person I am. It's true that half of me is a little bit pleased, but the other half wants to jump out of a window. What did I do right? What did I do wrong? What on earth made this happen to me? This has blown it. I'm leaving.

26

Goodbyes

I told the personnel woman that, although I was very sad about it, I was going to have to leave the Academy. Her face displayed a flash of quite authentic disappointment. I was really touched. I said I'd be off at the end of the week (temps can behave in this rash way – it's one of our only perks). I would probably have left today, but Philip is still away and I really want to say goodbye before I disappear. I hope he comes back tomorrow. It's strange, but he is the person at the Academy to whom I've become the most attached.

When other people leave they get given tea and cakes in the library. I've only been here for about four months, so I guess this won't happen. I have also only given them forty-eight hours' notice. Maybe they'll give me a card with all their signatures and best wishes and kisses. I think I'd like it. I don't know what I'd do with it, but I imagine that if I put it in a box and found it twenty years later it would give me some kind of thrill. I wonder who I'll be in twenty years' time. I'd better not be a receptionist. Next week I'm going start being a private Art History tutor – I rang a number I got from the Yellow Pages, told them I was qualified and experienced and they gave me a job. I couldn't believe it. I just wrote down a list of potential jobs (including waitress and cleaner) in the morning, and got one in the afternoon. If it's this easy, why didn't I act sooner? I had no idea. It was so unproblematic that it felt like a bit of an anticlimax. They didn't bother with a stressful interview, or even a CV. What a bunch of cowboys. I'm already worrying about whether or not it will turn out to be any more fulfilling than this job. All it involves is traipsing round houses in Knightsbridge telling bored adolescents why the Impressionists were so radical or what was so great about the king picking up Tintoretto's paintbrush. It happened so easily I can't believe it's true. Maybe they are going to kidnap me and sell me as a slave. Teaching is not something I ever saw myself doing, but I'm sure it won't be for ever. I like the idea of a job where people have to listen to what I say (and perhaps even take notes!) but I hate the idea of turning up at rich people's houses and being paid to get their thick, unmotivated brats into the 'right' universities. At the beginning I remember saying that one of my main aims was to get out of here, but now I'm wondering why. What's so bad about answering phones for a living? Why should it be worse than talking to rich teenagers about Renaissance painting? Or selling shares, or editing newspapers, or photographing food, or breeding cats, or producing TV programmes, or marrying a millionaire, or designing bridges, or boxing, or any of the other things people have to do to make sure they don't die of malnutrition in the short time they have on this planet?

One stupid problem I have is that I feel like I need to do something people will remember me for after I'm dead. I don't even believe in heaven, so I can't see why it should matter. Maybe it's just a silly way of trying to compensate for the meaninglessness of it all. It feels like an embarrassingly outdated preoccupation, but I don't care, I've got it. My new job won't help with this any more than the one I have now. What should I do to guarantee myself a place in history? Maybe I could do it by becoming Temp of the Month every month for ten years and going down as the best receptionist in the history of the world. I don't think this is something I could seriously be proud of. That's a good sign. At least it means I'm more interested in the things I have to do than in fame or notoriety itself. I am definitely not a person who could sit in a bath of baked beans for six months to get in the *Guinness Book of Records.* (And I'm really going to try not to do anything vile or terrible either.) I wonder who'll fare better in terms of sticking around in the far distant future, the ex-receptionist or me. I can't imagine, but I'm sure we're at least at level pegging with the Director.

Is the point behind all this morbid stuff something about the sense the ending gives to the whole? I'm about to stop being a receptionist in favour of something (slightly) preferable. (It pays fourteen pounds an hour, so it will only take me one hundred and twenty-eight thousand five hundred and seventy-four minutes to earn a thriller's worth of cash.) But what will happen after that and after that and after that? Who will I seem to have been when I die? What if I die before I realize my potential? What if I don't get a chance to turn into the person I believe I ought to because time and worldly things get in the way? How can I possibly know who I am until I drop dead, by which time it's too late? I really am pleased about quitting this job, but it's making me think very hard about what I should do in the future. I have no intention of staying a private tutor all my life. I'd love to be a bio-ethics consultant, but I'd have to go back to school all over again.

I suppose I have to start living in a way that I'd like to be remembered for instead of in a way that I can't wait to forget. Is this a good way to construct a satisfactory present for myself? Perhaps I should stop asking dumb questions. I think I should just get on with doing whatever I feel like, and seeing where it gets me. Well, the first step in that direction was leaving this job. So far, so good. I can be such a misery guts sometimes. Hooray for Art History. Hooray for teachers. Hooray for not being a receptionist any more. (Existential crisis averted.)

And then there's my love-life – an equally important endeavor. This, at least, is going very well. The MWM has even suggested that I stay with him while I decide what to do about my housing problems. I'm rather afraid of the outdoor bathroom facilities but it's a nice offer anyway. If someone had told me as little as four weeks ago that this might happen, I would have laughed and said it was out of the question.

But . . . Why is there always a downside with me? When I'm with the ⋀⋀⋀, being liked, I couldn't be happier. It's a thrill to be in my body with all those love-chemicals racing round my blood, making me feel warm and gushy. But when I leave and get to work I come over all crippled with doubt. I hate saying goodbye and often I feel like I do it so horribly that I make people want never to see me again. The worst goodbyes happen when you leave to do something you don't want to. This type generally turn out terribly because you have something else to blame – this vile commitment is forcing you to leave against your will. But so passionately wanting not to go makes you feel a little pathetic so you try to hide it but you can't completely, meaning that, more often than not, this reason for leaving brings about a goodbye that is ridiculous in its visible struggle between being cool and being devastated. It's also bad because it makes you rabid to get one last compliment or bit of affirmation from the person before you disappear, but you make it very hard for them to give it to you by acting a bit reserved ♥ and withdrawn. I always want to be told that everything's okay, and even the best possible kiss won't do because kisses don't have real endings (you just stop when either or both or sometimes neither of you feel like it) meaning that they can feel a bit broken-off and sad and futile. At moments like this I think you can make things better with a bit of verbal declaration – just because it's possible to construct a sentence so that it gives the impression of being a complete unit, meaning that whatever feeling it aims to transmit has slightly more chance of appearing to arrive intact than it does when packed into a kiss.

Maybe I'd learn to say goodbye better if I had a job I liked.

I can't believe I'm sitting here feeling terrible after a few days of really incredible bliss all because saying goodbye gives me such a huge shot of anxiety. This anxiety is a direct product of my frequent inability to show feelings straightforwardly, but I'm still unconvinced that blurting stuff out all the time is a great solution. I really admire it and like to try it once in a while, but I'm not sure that in the long run it makes you any happier. I suppose it depends on whether happiness is more likely to be brought about by making certain you get what other people think you want, or by knowing what you want irrespective of whether or not you get it. Tactical manoevres seem more suited to the first and tactless ones to the second. I sway far more towards the first one (and hate it) and my friend just swung me round to the second one (and I liked it) and now I'm all confused because, having had such a good time, I feel excessively terrible. I really am losing the plot.

27

Résumé

And, on the subject of plot, how about a quick résumé? What on earth is going on? What was going on before? I met the ⋀⋀⋀, didn't like him, then did like him, then got a stupid job, then lost him and went round the bend, then found him and didn't like him, then stopped hating the job, then started to like him again, then really fell for him, and then quit the job – which was meant to constitute a happy ending only it doesn't. Or perhaps it does. In its reduced form it reminds me a little bit of Cinderella – only I am both the prince who searches and the girl who does dull chores, while the ⋀⋀⋀ doubles as the charming gentleman and the vanishing love-object.

I think I might be having one of those moments like when you're trying to solve a puzzle and suddenly find that, while you were concentrating on getting one bit right, all the other bits have accidentally fallen into place (this happened to me a couple of times with a Rubik cube). You've finished the whole thing without actually discovering the secret of what made finishing possible.

I feel like I can't go on. It's finished. Conditions have changed so much and in such a favourable way that I no longer have the time nor the urge to write about the ⋀⋀⋀. I'm so pleased just to see him that I needn't supplement it with all this angst-ridden explanatory stuff. I am also about to start a job where I actually have to *do* something. This has come as quite a surprise to me. I don't quite know what I expected to happen. I think I saw myself getting stuck as a receptionist for quite a bit longer.

I also expected the whole love thing to end rather tragically without changing too much first. I guess it sounds like I'm saying I don't need *you*, but that's definitely not at all the way it's intended. It's been really helpful to have a place to spill everything out.

I don't know what you wanted but I fear it wasn't this. Perhaps you only carried on reading because you thought I was going to be punished or taught a serious lesson. But, in the case of the latter, I think I was. It seems to me that I landed myself with some kind of romantically inspired nervous illness and somehow I've recovered. I'm tempted to say this fantastic change is mysterious and leave it at that, but why not *try* to explain how this 'cure' came about (for future reference)? Really, it's the least I can do.

The *real* ending began to take shape around the time of the flat loss, the friend's benevolent interference and my announcement that the boyfriend and I had separated, after which things got better and better. Suddenly I could talk and all the bilge swimming round in my skull had a place to go rather than slopping around my cranium until it got so annoying I had to start writing it down. It's a typical result of this sort of good fortune. When you can actually talk, writing becomes a bit superfluous. Plato apparently believed that speech was a kind of instantaneous reading aloud of what he called 'the writing in the soul'. He also said that copying out the writing was a poor option reserved only for when there was no one around to hear you. Plato was obviously a deeply confused person but he has a point. With the ᴧᴧᴧ to speak to I'm less inclined to pick up my pen. I find conversation more fulfilling – he answers back, gives me different ways to think about things, pulls faces, touches me and generally affects me in ways that I like. I'm sure if I was talking to you it would be great, but this book-writing business has just become a nuisance.

Aside from not having to be writing a novel any more, the biggest improvement is that I no longer feel crazy and detached from everyone and everything but feel quite capable of dealing with life in all its intricacy and difficulty and even enjoying it. I feel like an alert and active person who can act on things and not someone who needs to open a vein in order to solve a problem. The MMM now seems to me a complicated, astute and thoughtful character. He's no longer a terrifying blank, but someone I speak to and who speaks back, who I listen to and who listens back. And it all works out much better than it did before. I think when I met him he was even more mixed up than I was, what with his pennilessness, homelessness and undecidedness about where to go. Because I was so afraid of the feelings I was having about him I couldn't really help him out.

One big relief is that this new state of affairs is even more compelling than the old one and I don't miss the excessive emotions and the torment at all. I can still feel tormented (now I really do have something to lose) but it's part of the rest of my existence and not a momentary dropping out into something else. If I don't understand the MMM, I ask him a question and believe that he'll answer it as well as he can. Some really weird things change when all this starts to happen. The stuff you can do splits off in two different directions. You start finding you can go to the supermarket together at the same time as you can disclose your biggest secrets and unveil your least presentable wishes. It's excellent. But instead of getting carried away by my own cheerfulness (which is only really entertaining for me) I'm supposed to be trying to work out what's going on with this thing of having and not having and going mad and getting sane again. It seems amazing to me that someone I barely knew, who I'd cried on once, could disappear to such devastating effect. What was it in him that made his vanishing act so disconcerting? People come and go all the time without me even noticing. Why should one person manage to stand out so dramatically from the rest? I know I said the thing he did that set it all off was pretty outstanding, but let's get this into perspective. He didn't save a drowning granny or donate an organ to an acquaintance or turn his house into a shelter for refugees. He just kind of communicated something rather obliquely (and publicly) that seemed to me to mean more than perhaps it should have. I almost forgot to tell you what it was, although it may sound so stupid you won't believe me anyway. He made a video of someone's feet running around on top of hundreds of neatly arranged examination tables in very noisy shoes. It was shown on a circle of screens lurking under a very high and very unstable-looking pile of plastic school chairs bound together with wire. The changing light from the screens made the shadows of the chairs move around all over the walls, giving you the feeling that they were falling down. The sound of clattering footsteps was pretty panic inducing, but the running person kept squealing every now and then as if they were having a really good time, and changing direction chaotically all over the neat grid. I guess what it seemed to me to be saying was, however bad your set-up is – like in a rigid, institutional hell where all your options appear to have been reduced to nothing – there is always something else you can do. No matter how bad things are looking it may still be possible to work out a way to enjoy yourself. I was feeling pretty gloomy about my alternatives at the time, so it was a big thrill to be reminded that there might be ways of dealing with them other than just getting depressed. (It's strange that after being so excited in front of the videos, I was so annoyed about the desk-jumping incident at the Academy. Sometimes reality can be so slow to catch up with ideas.)

Another possibility – in opposition to the nice, humanitarian one I have just given – was that the yelping woman, the tied-up furniture and even the schoolroom scene evoking restraint and the possibility of punishment was pretty sexy. Maybe it gave me the idea that he could get quite mean in the bedroom.

Whatever, the dumb truth is that I fell in love with him after crying in front of his work. Crying in shows and books and films is weird. It definitely points up how much you're prepared to go along with fictional things. It also makes you notice how hard it can be to tell the difference sometimes. I liked the ᴧᴧᴧᴧ's artwork, so I fell in love with him. A friend of mine, not famous for her intellect, asked me at her own wedding whether fiction was the one that was true or the other way round. I guess I know what she means now.

I feel very ashamed talking about all this because art can seem so unheroic. Maybe I wanted you to imagine that he had done something very serious in the real world. But in a roundabout way, he had. He produced an effect (on me) that has since produced effects elsewhere (on my ex-boyfriend, on the place where I work, on other people who saw the show, maybe even on you – you were reading, you missed your tube stop, were late for work one time too many, were fired, lost your home and died in a hostel in King's Cross) and now these effects will produce other effects, which will produce other effects, and who knows what will happen? With his work the ᴧᴧᴧᴧ has certainly changed the world.

Whatever it was I saw in his exhibition hit me a bit like the postcard – only better. And I think that may be a clue to the lunacy part. (I'm having my Poirot moment at last, it's really coming together. I just hope I can tell you quickly before I start losing the thread.) If the postcard told me about something that had been there and then disappeared (my parents) and explained my entire character to me, the ᴧᴧᴧᴧ's artwork made something seem to be there, in him (where it hadn't been before), and then he removed it by removing his entire person. This removal of something mirrored the removal of whatever had seemed to be there in my parents' bodies and, despite my newly developed adult character, sent me spinning off into childlike incomprehension. The world seemed as nonsensical to me as it must have seemed on my first birthday when those old bastards went off on their holiday. Only this time, in my more powerful adult state, I could try to do something about it – i.e. pursue and seduce the missing object in an attempt to get it back to where I wanted

182

it. Am I making sense? To put it another way, the postcard was excessively significant because of the way it signified something being (or having been) missing, while the table-jumping video stood out because it signified something suddenly appearing, as if from nowhere. This something, whatever it was, instantly became quite indispensable, making its disappearance feel as dreadful as my parents' inexplicable departure. I don't know. I suppose I haven't really got it any more worked out than I did at the beginning. Basically, it just drives you nuts when someone you have strong feelings about gives you the impression that they aren't quite so keen on you. It's one of those sublime injustices that you can't possibly get your head around even though it's a fairly common phenomenon.

What I am hoping is that the similarity between the two events will turn out to be the key to everything. The table-jumping story is like the postcard story in reverse. I want to imagine that, like in children's programmmes where a spell can be undone by saying it backwards, I have been magically returned to the perfect being I was before everything went wrong. No longer will I be obliged to have stupid hairstyles, to talk endlessly to people I don't like, or to fail to form lasting attachments (I'm particularly interested in this one) but will increasingly find myself behaving in a singularly unfucked up way.

⌣

Does all this sound a bit bogus? Everbody knows that a cure by love doesn't last. Perhaps I'm too keen to neaten up the ends. I think I may be suffering an outburst of literary politesse. I really want to give you a proper finale – I'm just not sure I can make one out of the raw materials I have.

Oh well. Poirot's solutions generally sound a bit rickety too (although he always turns out to be right).

⌣

I just got a really perfect farewell card from the Academy – but no tea and cakes. The card had a picture of water lilies on it and said something about my new career bringing me lots of Monet. The office manager said that she couldn't understand why I was leaving when I seemed to be just about getting the hang of the job. What a witch. She ought to thank me for sparing her life. The would-be-fireman could hardly look me in the face all day, and has just gone home without saying goodbye. I'd like to leave him an encouraging note, but perhaps he wouldn't like it. The nice membership lady seems very pleased for me, and the accounts people keep wishing me luck, making me feel quite remorseful about all that rubbish I said about them at the beginning. The Doctors mostly haven't said anything – except one, who said something really, really nice. She said she had seen me kissing the MMM at the end of the street after work, and it had made her laugh because she was about to meet her husband a bit further down the road in order to do the same thing. She said she had been married for twenty-five years and still got really excited when he came to meet her. She also said that waking up next to him was one of her favourite things in life. She made me feel very optimistic about the possibility of falling lastingly in love.

One minor tragedy was that I didn't get to say goodbye to Philip. I'm sure I'm just being silly, but I feel a bit bad for leaving without knowing whether or not he's okay. I saw how carelessly the Academy let Heck go. I do worry a little that if anything had happened to Philip no one here would be too bothered about it. But I guess it's not my business any more.

The other regret I have about leaving the Academy so suddenly is that I never managed to find out what the scary salesman was up to. (So not all the parts of this story have ended at once.) Maybe I will recognize him in the papers one day. Or perhaps his reappearance will make a climatic event in the new receptionist's tale.

*　　*　　*

So, is this a proper happy ending? I suppose it's possible. I think it's another one of those cases where you'd know better than me. I'm sure this feeling of completion won't go on for ever but, for now, I feel like succumbing to the illusion. I wonder how long you think it will last.

It's strange. Something in this knot of infantile abandonment and adult recuperation has made me really want to have a baby. ☎ (Look! A phone call! I had to tell you that the MMM just rang for NO REASON! – except to say that he couldn't wait for me to finish work. It's so easily the best reason of all. Now I feel quite certain that he loves me. I'm sickeningly saturated with delirious joy.) The MMM said today that he really wants one too, but we haven't yet discussed whether we'd like to have one with each other. Wouldn't it be odd if that was what happened? What on earth would it turn into? I bet it would look funny – Popeye with blonde ringlets and eyebrows that meet in the middle. And we'd have to take it with us *everywhere*, too. Shit.

⌒

So where does that leave you?[1] I can't imagine. I hope you don't feel conned. I mean everything happened like I promised it would at the beginning, but things are almost always different than the way you picture them in advance. What I didn't know back then was that writing was one of my symptoms. It's unhealthy to need to record everything you do. I'm going stick to holiday snaps and the occasional letter in future.

It's five o'clock and I can hear the hum of the lift. It must be the night porter. I can't believe I won't be coming back to the Academy next Monday. I wonder whether they'll survive without me. I doubt I'll ever bother to check.

[1] I just thought I'd use every last opportunity to communicate my gratitude before we part. Thanks.

Stop Press

Shit! Bloody hell! My hands are shaking so much I can hardly write. I'm on the tube too, which isn't helping. Oh Jesus! Fucking hell!!!! Shit!!!!!!!!!!

Something so outrageously terrible is going on I can hardly believe it. I didn't mean to carry on writing, but this is just too serious to skip. I got halfway down the road away from the Academy when I remembered the package I had hidden under the desk. I got so scared that the office manager might find it after I had gone that I went back to pick it up and chuck it in the bin at the end of the street. I don't know why I did it because she won't be able to tell me off from now on anyway. I walked back into the Academy, told the night porter that I had left something behind, and stuffed the parcel into my bag. When I got to the bin I realized I couldn't bear to throw it out without looking inside first. I thought it might contain vital notes detailing an invention of critical importance for the well-being of future generations. Or maybe a sample of an entirely new and revolutionary substance. Or just a pile of crap, in which case I wouldn't need to feel guilty about binning it.

Come on you pissy old train!

I slid my fingers under the tape and wrenched the box open. There was a bundle of stuff all wrapped in tissue-paper and cellophane. I unravelled it carefully and out came some different sized metal rings joined by bits of chain and a tiny bunch of keys. It was extremely shiny and light and was probably made from reinforced aluminium. I don't think I would necessarily have

186

realized what it was if the largest of the metal rings hadn't had two-inch long spikes on it. Without these it might have passed for a routine piece of engineering equipment. As it stood, you definitely didn't need an MA in Punishment to see that this was a rather serious-looking piece of bondage apparatus. I was so amazed I just stood there staring at it until I heard footsteps coming towards me and quickly stuffed it back into my bag.

I went to a nearby café to calm down and process the information, and after about one sip of cappuccino it dawned on me: Sir L. L. Lippoch was none other than Philip bloody Scroll. I remembered our lunchtime chats and the suspicious black door incident. It was so obvious I couldn't believe I hadn't worked it out before. It's the oldest trick in the book. The guy orders stuff through the mail and changes his name around so it can't be traced back to him. But why had he gone to all that effort and then not bothered to follow it up? Maybe he didn't want the gadget any more. Maybe he forgot. It's true that I only asked the secretaries about Lippoch and never any of the Doctors in person. Maybe he knew it had arrived but was anxious I may have checked inside when I didn't recognize the name. Perhaps he had a more efficient arrangement with the ex-receptionist. What a nut.

When I made the connection between him and the gadget I got really, really full-scale worried again. The guy is a miserable, lonely bachelor into some kind of heavy sex scene and his mother, who may be the only friend he has, is about to pop her clogs – if she hasn't done it already. I knew I had to go and check that he was okay.

Come on! Oh shit! We've stopped in a fucking tunnel!

The only way I could think of to get hold of him without telling anybody why I urgently needed his address was to go back to the stupid old Academy *again* and try to get his number from the personnel woman's office. I was beginning to fear I might never be able to escape because every time I thought I'd gone for good I'd have to go back on some other ludicrous errand. I was scared I'd end up stuck there forever like the would-be-fireman. I knew for sure that the personnel lady had left as I'd seen her go before me, but I wasn't sure about all the secretaries and accounts people on her floor. I walked back in for the second time and told the night porter I had left my make-up in the loo. I got into the lift, but instead of going down to the toilets I went up to the second floor. It was the first time I had ever been upstairs and I had no idea where to start looking. I turned to the left and crept down the corridor. It was a real shock to see the office. The reception is always the best designed part of any organization. Once you get properly inside all offices look disgusting. In contrast to the chandeliers, marble and ceiling roses I associated with the Academy, upstairs was just your regular grey-carpeted, formica-shelved, paper mountain. No wonder the office manager got embarrassed about the Queen's husband coming round.

I heard a keyboard clacking in one of the rooms near the end of the corridor. I was about to scuttle back in the other direction when I noticed that the door right at the end had the personnel lady's name on it. If I could only get past the typing person I guessed I should be able to manage it. I sneaked down as quietly as I could and peeped in the doorway to check who was there. It was pretty horrible, to tell the truth. The large accounts lady and her tiny husband were in there together. He was sitting on her lap and typing. They seemed to be concentrating quite hard on whatever they were working on, so I just slipped past and into the room at the end. Happily, the personnel lady had a Rolladex right in the middle of her desk. I went straight to S and got Philip's address, but no phone number. I bet he doesn't even have a phone, the mopey old sod.

I raced out of the Academy without bothering too much about being sneaky. I decided to make this the last time I would ever, ever need to go there.

So here I am on a bloody train to Cockfosters going out of

my mind with worry about someone I don't even know and writing in my dumb notebook again like a nutter even though I promised myself I'd stop. It's incredible what stupid directions your life can take if you're not careful.

⌒

Well, that was an experience. I got to Cockfosters and took about ten minutes to find Philip's house – which was about one minute away from the station. The thing that started to worry me even more than all the bloodthirsty stuff was that he would be perfectly okay, sitting in the living room watching telly with a cup of tea. He would wonder why on earth I had suddenly appeared on his doorstep, all out of breath and crazy. Would I tell him I knew about Sir L. L. Lippoch? Or just let him believe I knew nothing and make up some crappy story about how I happened to be passing? I almost got back on the tube for fear of completely shaming myself.

When I finally found Philip's front door, I stood in front of it for about a minute psyching myself up. What was I about to discover (or not)? I rang the doorbell.

There was a load of barking and the sound of dog claws scrabbling around on lino. I waited and he didn't come. He was probably at the hospital with his mother. I couldn't decide whether to drop a note in or to forget it and go home. The dogs were barking like mad. I couldn't bear to have come all this way for nothing. I decided to ring the bell one more time, just in case. I buzzed and the dogs went even more nuts. They started yowling and yelping and jumping up at the letterbox. I stood back and looked up just in time to see a curtain twitching upstairs. I yelled out Philip's name. I was definitely getting the impression that something was up. I waited a bit longer and Philip's forehead and eyes appeared in the bottom corner of the upstairs window. I didn't know how to act, so I smiled stupidly and waved. What the fuck was he doing up there? I

189

called out to ask if he would let me in. He shook his head. I guessed I must have come at a bad moment. Maybe he had someone else there. He didn't look very happy though. Insofar as I could tell from the tiny bit of face he was showing, he looked very disturbed. I asked him if *I* was disturbing him and he shook his head again. He was really being a pain in the arse. Why didn't he at least pretend to be a bit pleased I'd come over? I asked him whether his mother was okay and this time he paused, nodded and disappeared. I sat on the wall and waited to see what he'd do next.

About three minutes later there was a knocking from the inside of the front door. I rushed over. The dogs had gone all soft and whimpery. I banged back and said hello a couple of times. There was a tiny bark and then another banging coming from the bottom part of the door. I crouched down and tried a bit more helloing. Then I heard Philip's voice, only it sounded all funny like there was something wrong with his mouth. I tried to work out what he was saying but all I could make out were the words 'flower pot'. It seemed perfectly clear that the guy had flipped. He carried on saying 'flower pot' a few more times so, out of respect, I looked around for a flower pot. The only one he had was a small geranium over in the corner by the bin. I listened again to see if he'd changed the subject and he said the word 'key'.

I would make a terrible burglar. Half the world keeps a front door key under a bloody geranium but even in the direst emergency it would never occur to me to look there. I rushed over to the pot and got the key out from underneath. I jammed it into the lock and threw the front door open.

I didn't know whether to laugh or scream. Curled in a ball on the floor, surrounded by four yapping Jack Russells, was a semi-naked and super-skinny Philip all tangled up in a mess of straps, studs, chains, padlocks and metal corsetry, with something like a horse's bit in his mouth. He looks sheepish and embarrassed at the best of times, but today he was really going for it. When I bent down to ask him what had happened he burst into tears.

It transpired that he had been trying something out for the first time (or so he claimed) and had left the keys to the locks on the table by the side of his bed. One of the dogs had jumped up, knocked the tiny bunch of keys onto the floor and straight down a large crack between the floor-boards. How unlucky can you get? The harness was so ungainly – his feet were attached by two-foot chains to his neck and his hands were cuffed behind his back – that he didn't have a hope of lifting the boards by himself. I asked why he hadn't called the fire brigade and he flinched and shook his head.

Luckily it was a crusty old house and it didn't take more than two minutes to lever up the floor-board. I got him his dressing gown, handed him the keys and went into the kitchen to put the kettle on. It's funny how quickly you can get used to weird things. One minute I was on a train going bananas about what I was about to find. The next minute I was actually finding it. And then straight after that I was making myself at home in the kitchen. I think this feeling of normality was brought about by the fact that I wasn't altogether surprised about this sort of caper coming from Philip. To be frank, it actually arrived more as a confirmation.

His milk was a bit off after five or so days in the fridge so I made two black teas and went to wait for him in the sitting room. I heard talking sounds coming from upstairs. I guessed he was talking to his mother – so he *does* have a phone after all. She must have been pretty relieved to hear from him. He came down about ten minutes later, all dressed up like he was off to work. It was as if by changing his outfit he hoped to make me forget what I'd quite clearly witnessed just a short while before. I asked him about his mother and he said she was probably going to live this time but that she'd have to move to a nursing home. He went on and on about all the different nursing homes in his area and what was good and

191

bad about each of them. He didn't exactly spare any details. I realized that it was very unlikely I would ever really be able to be his friend.

After about half an hour spent listening to his well-meant but basically boring chit-chat I decided it was time to leave. I stood up and started to say goodbye before I remembered the package. Should I hand it over or not mention it? I looked around the living room. It was really badly decorated – all peely patterned wallpaper and threadbare furniture. I thought about the shiny aluminium harness in my bag. It must have been really expensive. It was quite an attractive object. It was certainly nicer that anything else I had seen in Philip's mouldy house. But what if he got himself in trouble again and I wasn't around to save him? You could be sure that those old bastards back at the Academy would just let him rot.

Philip ventured something pathetic about how kind it was of me to come and see him. It annoyed me. I hadn't come to see him. I had probably saved his stupid life, only he couldn't admit it because he was too embarrassed.

I said I had brought him a present and his face kind of lit up. I put my hand in my bag and pulled out the gadget. He looked at me completely amazed and then gawped down at his toy. It was obvious he was thrilled. He hesitated, then picked it up and examined excitedly it like a child at Christmas. It was almost beautiful to see. I told him to look after himself and to keep the keys on a string tied to the bedpost. He thanked me rather bashfully. Then we shook hands, said goodbye and I left.

And now here I am again finishing my book. That's it this time, I promise. The Academy has been purged from my life. I'm glad I got to go upstairs before I left though. Bloody Philip, coming along and upstaging everyone at the last minute. What will the ∿∿∿ say? *He* was meant to be the star.

This was not the sort of ending I wanted for my book. It was meant to be quiet and thoughtful, not all action-packed and suspenseful. Oh well. Bollocks to it. Who am I to say what's meant to happen? Who knows? Thanks to Philip I may be one step nearer to that £30,000. At least I'll know what to get him as a thank you gift.

Anyhow, no more encores this time. I'm hanging up.

Douglas Coupland

Microserfs

'About as Zeitgeisty as it gets.' *GQ*

At computer giant Microsoft, Dan, Susan, Abe, Todd and Bug are struggling to get a life in a high-speed high-tec environment. The job may be super cool, the pay may be astronomical, but they're heading nowhere, and however hard they work, however many shares they earn, they're never going to be as rich as Bill. And besides, with all the hours they're putting in, their best relationships are on e-mail. Something's got to give ...

'A funny and stridently topical novel. Coupland continues to register the buzz of his generation.'

JAY MCINERNEY, *New York Times*

'The kooky aphoristic ripeness of Coupland's writing almost succeeds in making us forget the hollowness of these live-to-work lives. In the first 50 pages, there are more one-liners than in a decade of Woody Allen films.'

ROBIN HUNT, *Guardian*

'Coupland is the crowned king of North American pop culture.' *NME*

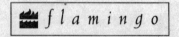 *flamingo*

Suzannah Dunn

Venus Flaring

'Suzannah Dunn is a gifted writer'   *The Times*

Ornella and Veronica are the very best of friends, inseparable throughout the trials and minute details of their lives, sharing everything, hiding nothing. They grow up and find their way into the world together – Ornella, flamboyant and domineering, becomes a doctor, Veronica, observant and self-possessed, a journalist. But then something goes horribly wrong between them, and what was once the truest of friendships disintegrates into an obsessive nightmare of smouldering resentment that can barely be controlled. As Ornella's loyalty fades, Veronica's desperate need for reconciliation becomes a matter of life and death – and if you can't trust your best friend with your life, then who can you trust?

In prose that soars and fizzes with startling truths, Suzannah Dunn has created a deliciously disturbing and stylishly compelling tale of loyalty, love, memory, obsession and ultimate betrayal.

'Dunn writes with a warm attentive style which makes her characters compellingly real.'   *Time Out*

'Suzannah Dunn writes in loaded and knowing prose, like a hip Edna O'Brien or Muriel Spark in a gymslip.'
                                                        Glasgow Herald

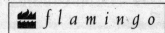 *flamingo*